Starting School

Starting School

Johanna Hurwitz

Illustrated by Karen Dugan

A
LITTLE
APPLE
PAPERBACK

SCHOLASTIC INC.

New York Toronto London Auckland Sydney
Mexico City New Delhi Hong Kong

Special thanks to Mrs. Jeanette Beard and her kindergarten students at
Monroe School in Janesville, Wisconsin, and to all the other kindergarten teachers
and children I've met in the past few years. Also thanks to Fain Dolinsky for
sharing family stories and for locating and mailing my computer disk to me
when I went off on vacation and left it behind.

ISBN: 0-439-17215-2

12 11 10 9 8 7 6 5   8 9/0

Printed in the U.S.A.   40

First Scholastic printing, September 2000

For my grandson
Ethan Alexander Richardson.
Welcome to the world!

Starting School

Contents

The First Day

It was the first Wednesday of September. Two young boys were about to start school. The boys were named Marcus and Marius Cott. They were five years old, and they were identical twins.

Even though they no longer dressed in matching clothes, the two brothers had exactly the same features, hair color, height, and weight. Mrs. Cott looked fondly at her two young sons during breakfast. "It's a good thing you're in different kindergarten classes," she said. "It would be hard work for a teacher to tell you apart."

"I can tell us apart," Marius responded at once. He looked across the table at his twin brother. "That's Marcus," he said, pointing.

"That's right," agreed Marcus. "I'm me. And he's not me. He's Marius," he added.

"I want to be in the same class with Marcus," Marius told his mother as he licked some bright red strawberry jam off his fingers. "We should be in the *same* kindergarten."

"And I want to be in Marius's class," said Marcus. One of his cheeks was shiny with butter. He didn't like jam on his toast. "I want to be in Marius's class," Marcus said again. He had a habit of repeating himself.

"You can't be in the same class. That's the school rule," their big brother, Lucas, explained to the boys. "Brothers and sisters can't be together. They won't even let cousins be in the same classroom." Lucas was in sixth grade, and he had been going to school since before the twins were born. He knew everything there was to know about Edison-Armstrong School.

"It won't be any fun if we're not together," said Marius. "We're always together."

"Always," Marcus echoed.

"Your classrooms are just across the hall from each other," Mrs. Cott explained. "And you're only going to school for half a day. By noon, you'll be together again and eating lunch right back here at this table."

"Good," said Marius, temporarily distracted by the thought of the afternoon meal. "What's for lunch?" he asked.

"You haven't finished breakfast yet," said Lucas. "What do you care about lunch?"

"It's *my* stomach, and *I* care," Marius replied.

"Tomato soup," said Mrs. Cott.

"Good," said Marius. These days, he only wanted to eat foods that were red.

Marius was the younger of the twins by twelve minutes. He was outspoken, and so people who didn't know the boys sometimes thought he was smarter. Usually, he was the leader in their games and mischief. Marcus, though quieter and more thoughtful, was equally bright.

Marius suddenly put down his piece of toast and stood up. "Listen, Lucas. I remember all those words you taught us," he said, putting his sticky hand across his chest.

"Me too. Me too," shouted Marcus when he saw what his twin was about to do. He jumped up and almost knocked over his glass of milk. Together the boys recited the words "I pledge allegiance to the flag of the United States..."

"Stop, stop," said their mother. "Save it until you get to school and you can tell your teacher. Sit down and finish your breakfasts. It's getting late."

"Which teacher do I have?" Marcus asked. "Which teacher is mine?"

Mrs. Cott looked at the letter she had received from the school. "Marcus Cott is in Ms. Boscobel's class. Marius Cott is in Mrs. Greenstein's class," she read.

"Boscobel. Boscobel," Marcus repeated, memorizing the new name.

"Mrs. Greenstein's class?" said Lucas. "She teaches in the *mouse room*."

"Mouse room?" asked Mrs. Cott, puzzled by this news.

"What's the mouse room?" asked Marius excitedly.

"There was a mouse in that room last year. Cricket knew someone who had a little sister in that class, and she saw it. Cricket told us all about it."

4

"I love mice," said Marius. Perhaps kindergarten had even more to offer than he had realized.

"That's good, because the room smells like them," said Lucas.

"Smells like mice? I want mice in my classroom," Marcus complained. "I love mice, too."

"I'm sure the school has gotten rid of the mice by now," said Mrs. Cott. She reached over with a wet paper towel and wiped Marcus's face. "Hurry up, fellows. Finish eating. You don't want to be late on your first day of school."

"This is the first day of my last year at Edison-Armstrong School," Lucas pointed out. He proudly put on the blue sash with the silver badge that showed he was a Safety Patrol monitor. It was his job to help students cross one of the streets near the school building. "I've got to run ahead, but I'll look for you when you get to school," he said to his brothers. He grinned at both boys. "You'll knock 'em dead!" he predicted.

Marcus watched enviously as Lucas ran off. He wished he was as big and smart as his older brother.

"We'd better start moving, too," Mrs. Cott

said, and led the twins toward the bathroom. There she supervised as they washed their hands. She recombed their hair and checked that they both went to the toilet.

Each of the boys had a new backpack. They had insisted they needed them. Didn't Lucas go to school every day with one slung over his shoulder? Unfortunately, neither Marcus nor Marius could think of anything to put inside their backpacks. But that didn't mean they were going to leave them at home.

"I know what," shouted Marius suddenly. Lucas always had books in his backpack. Marius ran to their bedroom and returned with a well-worn copy of *Curious George*.

"I need to put something in my backpack, too," shouted Marcus, and he ran upstairs to the bedroom.

"Hurry," called his mother. "We should have left the house by now."

"I'm coming," Marcus called, but he was still going in the wrong direction.

On the floor of the bedroom he shared with his twin brother was a deck of playing cards. He liked to put them in piles by number. And this morning when he first woke up he'd been doing just that. Marcus scooped up all the cards and stuffed them into their box. He'd bring the cards to school and show his new teacher that he could recite the numbers in order: one, two, three, four, and so on. He knew she'd admire how well he knew them all. On the other hand, Marcus wasn't sure counting was quite as impressive as finding a mouse in the classroom.

As he slipped the deck of cards into his backpack, Marcus had a thought. He raced downstairs and asked Marius a question.

"Do you think you'll be able to catch the mouse in your classroom? If you do, you can bring it home inside your backpack so we can play with it together."

"I'll catch the mouse," Marius said confidently.

"I wish I was going to be in the same room with you. Then we could look for the mouse together," Marcus said sadly as the boys and their mother set off for school. "I could help you."

Even though they'd gone to a preschool program the year before, the twins realized that this was a big milestone in their lives. The preschool had a baby name: Happy Times Play School.

The name Edison-Armstrong School sounded grown-up and important.

"Come on, fellows, walk briskly," their mother instructed. As they went, they saw other students on their way to school, too. A yellow school bus passed them on the street.

"I wish we could take the school bus," commented Marcus. "I wish we could take the school bus."

"We live too near the school for you to need a bus," said Mrs. Cott. "Besides, walking is good exercise."

"Running is better," said Marius, and he raced on ahead. Marcus ran to catch up with his twin.

"Wait at the corner!" shrieked Mrs. Cott.

The two boys halted and waited at the corner for their mother to reach them. Then together the three of them watched for the light to turn green.

"We know the way to school," said Marius as they walked along. "We could go to school alone, just like Lucas."

"Lucas is almost twelve years old," his mother reminded him. "You're still five."

"One, two, three, four, five!" shouted Marius.

"Very good," said Mrs. Cott.

"Six, seven, eight, nine, ten," Marcus added. "Eleven, twelve…"

Suddenly Marius recognized a girl who was walking toward the school, too. She was in Lucas's class.

"Hello, Cricket," said Mrs. Cott, greeting her. "I was sure you would be a Safety Patrol monitor like Lucas."

"I could have been a monitor. I would have been a monitor. In fact, I *should* have been a monitor," said Cricket, her voice rising in displeasure. "But they made the selections for the Safety Patrol in the spring, when I still had a cast on my ankle. Do you remember that I broke my ankle last April?"

"Yes, I do," said Mrs. Cott. "I'm glad to see you're just fine now."

"Mr. Herbertson, the principal, should have known I'd be okay by September," said Cricket with disgust. "Hey," she cried suddenly, looking down at her feet. "Stop that!"

Both Marcus and Marius were squatting down on the ground and poking at her ankles.

"What does a broken ankle look like?" Marius wanted to know.

"Get up at once, boys," said Mrs. Cott.

10

"I feel sorry for their teacher," said Cricket as the four of them continued toward the school.

"They're really lovely boys," said Mrs. Cott, defending the twins.

"I remember Lucas when he was in kindergarten. He was awful. And two Lucases would be even worse."

"Neither of these boys is Lucas," said Mrs. Cott. "This is Marcus and this is Marius. And they each have their own personalities and their own kindergarten teachers."

"Well, at least Mr. Herbertson didn't make a mistake by putting them both in the same classroom," said Cricket. "I would never want to be in the same class with two brothers of Lucas Cott."

"So what," said Marcus. And before he could repeat his words, his twin did it for him.

"So what," said Marius.

By this time, they had arrived at the old brick building. There were hundreds of children and parents on the street outside the school.

"Where's Lucas? We didn't see Lucas," shouted Marcus.

"I think his post is on the other side of the school," said Mrs. Cott. "Tomorrow, if we get here earlier, we'll go looking for him."

A loud bell rang, and suddenly the hundreds of voices cheered and moaned at the signal of the start of the new school year. "It's time to go inside now," said Mrs. Cott. "Enjoy sixth grade," she called to Cricket.

The older students lined up to enter the building. But the parents of the kindergarten children were expected to bring their youngsters inside the building on this first day of school. The two kindergarten classrooms were off on the right-hand wing of the building. Mrs. Cott took a hand of each of her sons and led them forward.

"Oh, yuck. What do I smell?" asked Marcus. "What do I smell?"

"You smell you," said Marius to his twin.

A man nearby was sweeping up some sawdust on the floor. He looked at Mrs. Cott and her sons and gave a shrug of his shoulders.

"There seems to be a rule or something. Every year one of those kindergarten kids throws up on the first day," he said.

"*These* kindergarten kids are not going to do that," said Mrs. Cott, looking anxiously at her sons.

"Well, welcome to your first day at school,"

the man greeted the boys. "My name is King," he said to them. "George. I'm the new custodian here. I used to work at Thomas Jefferson School, but I was transferred when the other fellow who worked in this building retired."

"Hi, King George. I'm Marius," said Marius.

"I'm Marcus, King George."

"King George. Say, I like that," said the custodian, standing a little taller as he went on with his work.

"We'll see you around," said Mrs. Cott, and continued walking with her two boys toward the kindergarten rooms. Mrs. Greenstein stood at the doorway greeting her new students.

"Which of you is in this class?" she asked, looking from one brother to the other.

"This is Marius," said Mrs. Cott, letting go of his hand.

"Hello, Marius," said Mrs. Greenstein with a broad smile. "Welcome to kindergarten."

"Did you see the mouse yet?" Marius asked his teacher.

"Mouse? What mouse?" asked Mrs. Greenstein.

"My brother said this is the mouse room. He

said you have a mouse in here," said Marius, looking into the room.

"No mice. Just lots of other boys and girls for you to meet," said Mrs. Greenstein, tucking a piece of her gray hair behind her ear.

"Oh," said Marius. He looked very disappointed, but he remembered Lucas's words and sniffed the air.

"It *does* smell like mice," he said, and a look of anticipation returned to his face.

"Good-bye, Marius," said Mrs. Cott. "I'll see you in a couple of hours."

Marcus grabbed Marius's arm. "Don't forget to bring the mouse home," he reminded his brother.

"I won't," said Marius, yanking at his backpack.

Reluctantly, Marcus followed his mother to Ms. Boscobel's room. It was right across the hall, just as Mrs. Cott had told her son it would be.

Marcus looked at his new teacher. She was prettier than Mrs. Greenstein, he thought as he let go of his mother's hand. He put his hand across his heart and began reciting slowly, "I pledge allegiance to the flag..."

Ms. Boscobel appeared very surprised.

"His older brother taught him all the words," Mrs. Cott explained to the teacher. "He said you needed to know the pledge if you were going to school."

"Don't say it now," said Ms. Boscobel, interrupting Marcus. "Later you can help me teach the other children," she added.

Marcus smiled proudly.

Mrs. Cott turned to go, but her son ran back to his mother and grabbed her hand. "What are you going to do now?" he wanted to know.

"I'm going home to clean up from breakfast and fix lunch," she explained. "I'll be back to pick you boys up before you know it."

"Okay," said Marcus. "Okay." He looked through the door into his classroom, where the other children were sitting on a rug on the floor. He could also see the shelves of books and toys inside. He was sorry that Marius wasn't there with him, but he thought his kindergarten class looked like it would be fun.

Inside the
Teachers' Room

It was the first Wednesday of September. Two kindergarten teachers had just taught the first session of their new morning classes. The teachers were named Mrs. Lillian Greenstein and Ms. Josephine Boscobel, sometimes called Josie for short. Although Mrs. Greenstein had been teaching for twenty years and Ms. Boscobel was only in her second year as a teacher, they both had similar comments and complaints to make.

"This morning was awful! It's a good thing I only have one of those Cott twins in my classroom," said Mrs. Greenstein, biting into the stalk of celery from her lunch. "I could never handle two of them. Despite all my years of teaching, I can barely manage *one*. Of course, they must have put the worst twin in my class since I'm a more experienced teacher."

"Don't talk," said Ms. Boscobel, who wasn't referring to the fact that Mrs. Greenstein had been speaking with food in her mouth. "I may be a relatively new teacher, but I doubt that there will ever be another child like Marcus Cott. I'm sure he is by far the more difficult of the two. It's only the first day of school and already he's driving me crazy. For some reason, he repeats everything he says. He even repeated whatever I said. I thought I'd go bananas."

"That's nothing," said Mrs. Greenstein. "Do you know what Marius did?" she asked as she opened her container of strawberry-flavored yogurt. "He spent almost the entire morning crawling along the floor in the classroom. He couldn't be distracted by *any* of the games or activities."

"At least he didn't disrupt the rest of the class," said Ms. Boscobel.

Mrs. Greenstein swallowed a mouthful of

yogurt. "But he did! He said his older brother told him that there was a mouse in my classroom last year. Before I knew it, half the children were crawling along on their hands and knees looking for a mouse hole."

"There *was* a mouse in your room last year," Ms. Boscobel recalled.

"Don't remind me of that," said Mrs. Greenstein, shuddering. "Mr. Herbertson promised me that an exterminator went through the school during the summer and that we're free of all pests."

"I guess he wasn't referring to any of the students." Ms. Boscobel giggled.

"The worst thing is that Marius found two different places in the wall that certainly appear to be potential mouse holes. He claims that he could smell the mice inside the walls. So then all the children in my class began sniffing the air. Now half the class is eagerly watching for a mouse to appear and the other half is terrified."

"You can't blame Marius for discovering holes that actually exist in the walls," Ms. Boscobel said, defending the boy who was not in her class.

"Well, all I can say is that a little later, I was

reading a story to the children and there was a tiny sound in the room. Two girls and one boy jumped up and ran to me shouting, 'It's the mouse! It's the mouse!'"

"The next time they think they hear a mouse, tell your children it's Mickey Mouse. No one's afraid of him," suggested Ms. Boscobel.

A beep from the microwave oven indicated that Ms. Boscobel's bowl of tomato soup was ready for her to eat.

"Listen to this," said Ms. Boscobel, breaking some crackers into her soup. "This is what a real problem is: Marcus had a box of playing cards."

"What's wrong with that?" asked Mrs. Greenstein.

"He took them out of their box and said, 'My brother Lucas taught me a special game. It's called fifty-two pickup.' And with that, he threw the entire deck in the air. Of course, every child in the room went running to pick up the cards. Each one wanted to see how much of the deck he or she could get. It was wild. And naturally, in the midst of that, who should walk into the room but Mr. Herbertson."

"He does have a knack for showing up at the moment when you would least like to see the

school principal," agreed Mrs. Greenstein.

"Somehow I managed to collect all the cards and to get the students to sit quietly on the floor. Then I introduced Mr. Herbertson to them. Everyone else looked at him quietly in awe, but not Marcus. He called out a couple of questions."

"What did he want to know?" asked Mrs. Greenstein.

"He said 'When did you buy this school?' and 'Did it cost a lot of money?'"

The two women were laughing as the door opened and several other teachers walked into the room to join them for lunch.

"You seem pleased with your new classes," commented a third-grade teacher named Mrs. Hockaday.

"Pleased?" gasped Mrs. Greenstein.

"Pleased?" echoed Ms. Boscobel.

"Please. I'll need a lifetime's supply of aspirin if my afternoon group is anything like the morning one," said Mrs. Greenstein.

"You'll get them all trained before you know it," Mrs. Hockaday comforted the two kindergarten teachers.

"This is only the first day," said another teacher.

"That's right. Just one hundred eighty more days before summer vacation," said another.

Mrs. Greenstein and Ms. Boscobel looked at each other and sighed. It was going to be a long school year.

Mrs. Greenstein's Class

Every day, every hour, every minute, awake and asleep, for his entire life up until now, Marius had been together with his brother Marcus. They ate, played, bathed, dressed, and slept side by side.

Last year, when they went to preschool, Marius and Marcus had been in the same class. Sometimes during small-group activities, their teacher tried, unsuccessfully, to separate them. But she found they worked well with each other, so she gave in, and the boys continued to play and work side by side.

During the first few mornings at Edison-Armstrong School, Marius kept looking over his shoulder for his twin. Where was Marcus? What was he doing? he wondered. But each time as he looked around, he remembered again that Marcus was off in a different room, in a different group, with a different teacher. It was almost as if he had lost his own shadow.

Still, Marius enjoyed kindergarten. He liked the other children in his class. There were so many of them: Cole, Travis, Jonah, and Eric were the names of some of the boys. And among the girls, he counted off Kayla, who had red hair, Avery Goodman, whose name really spelled out *A very good man* (even though she was a girl), Jenna, who sucked her thumb, and two Jessicas. There were a couple of other girls, too, but Marius forgot their names.

Poor Mrs. Greenstein forgot everybody's name frequently during the first days. She called all the girls Jessica. With two of them in the class it meant that she was right sometimes. She also got the boys mixed up. But for some lucky reason, she always remembered Marius's name. That proved how much she liked him, he decided.

On the second morning of kindergarten, Marius was delighted to see his brother Lucas walk into Mrs. Greenstein's room.

"Lucas!" he shouted with excitement, and raced toward him. He acted as if he hadn't seen his brother in years and years, instead of just an hour earlier at home.

Lucas slapped his brother on the back and walked over to Mrs. Greenstein to give her a note.

Marius's teacher read it quickly and nodded her head. "Boys and girls, give me your attention," she called out. "This is Lucas Cott from the sixth grade," she announced when everyone was quiet and looking at her. "He has a message for all of us."

"He's my brother!" Marius called out proudly.

Lucas grinned at Marius. Then he spoke in a loud and important voice, different from the way he spoke at home. "The sixth grade is starting a clothing drive."

"I love drives," Marius called out. "Where are we going?"

"It's not that kind of a drive," said Lucas, looking at Marius and using his ordinary voice. He turned to look at the other children, and he explained, "A clothing drive means that we're going to give clothes to families that need help. Bring your clothing to school. There will be big boxes in the entrance of the building, and you can put the clothing in them."

"Here," Marius called out. His voice was muffled by his T-shirt, which was halfway over his head. "You can have this old shirt of mine," he offered.

"Marius. Put your shirt back on," both Mrs. Greenstein and Lucas said at the same time.

"I want to go on the clothing drive," said Marius.

"The clothing that you donate must come from home," said Mrs. Greenstein.

"This shirt came from home," Marius insisted.

"It has to come from home and you can't be wearing it," Lucas tried explaining.

"I'm not wearing it!" shouted Marius triumphantly. "See. I'm not wearing it." Marius stood bare-chested, holding out his T-shirt to his brother.

"You're going to catch a cold," said Mrs. Greenstein. "Stop. Stop," she called out. Two other boys were beginning to remove their shirts, too.

"We only want clothing that you've out-grown," Lucas tried to explain further as Mrs. Greenstein rushed to help the children redress themselves. "Especially sweaters and warm jackets for the winter."

Marius reluctantly put his shirt back on. He was disappointed that there wasn't going to be a bus or a car to go for a drive in. Still, it had been fun to have his brother come visiting in his class-room.

The first week of kindergarten was passing quickly. On Friday morning, Mrs. Greenstein called out, "Marius. What are you doing on the floor again? You were looking at a book in the reading corner a moment ago."

Marius had been hunting once again behind the wooden blocks on the bottom shelf of the block corner. He was still searching for the mouse that Lucas had told him about. Yesterday he had crumbled two vanilla wafers left over from snack time and dropped the pieces behind the blocks. He wondered if the mouse had found them during the night. If the cookie crumbs were gone, it would mean that the mouse had a good snack time, too.

"Did you find the mouse yet?" asked Cole

eagerly. He knew what Marius was doing down on the floor even if their teacher wasn't sure. Cole dropped to the floor near Marius and started looking, too.

"There is no mouse in this room," Mrs. Greenstein said sternly. "Now, Marius, get up from the floor and go sit on a chair in the library corner. And Cole, you're supposed to be working on your letters at the writing table."

Marius got up from the floor. He liked the library corner, with the many picture books on display. He could always look for the mouse later on.

Marius picked out one of the books and sat down in a small rocking chair. The book was *If You Give a Mouse a Cookie*. Marius knew the entire story by heart. He turned the pages rapidly and went to get another book. It was also one that he was familiar with, *Make Way for Ducklings*. Again, he turned page after page. When he jumped up to get a third book, Mrs. Greenstein stopped him.

"You can't rush through those books so quickly," she said. "If you turn the pages that fast, you don't get a chance to see anything."

"I saw everything," Marius insisted.

"Turn the pages and look at this book again," said the teacher. "It's about a family of little baby ducks."

"I know all about it," said Marius, but he sat down in the rocking chair and turned the pages once again.

Mrs. Greenstein watched Marius. "That's much more like proper kindergarten behavior," she complimented her student. "Give yourself a big pat on the back."

Those were the words Mrs. Greenstein always used when she was pleased with someone. Marius grinned, and resting the book on his lap, he reached with his right hand and patted himself.

In a little while it was time for the morning snack. "Make way for Marius," Marius shouted as he charged toward the table with his classmates. Every day the children had a small cup of fruit juice and a cookie or cracker. Today the snack was pretzels and apple juice.

Marius quickly ate his pretzel and looked around for more. Some of the children were licking the salt off their pretzels, but he had nothing left to eat. "Look at me," he called out. He climbed up onto the table and grabbed his left ankle with his right hand and his right ankle with his left hand and walked about that way.

"I'm a pretzel!" he announced proudly.

"Marius. What in the world do you think you're doing?" scolded Mrs. Greenstein. "I don't know where you learned a trick like that."

"My brother Lucas taught Marcus and me to be pretzels," Marius said.

"Well, get down at once and start acting like a graham cracker," said Mrs. Greenstein.

"How does a graham cracker act?" Marius asked.

"It sits quietly and minds its own business," said Mrs. Greenstein.

Marius untwisted himself and began getting down off the table. As he lowered his foot, he accidentally knocked over the cup of apple juice belonging to one of the Jessicas. None of the juice got on Marius, but it spilled on the table and some of the juice landed in Jessica's lap.

"Don't fuss," said Mrs. Greenstein quickly. She handed over some paper napkins so the spilled juice could be mopped up. "Now you see what happens when you don't sit properly," she said to Marius.

After snack time, Mrs. Greenstein gathered

the students on the carpet. "Today we're going to review the days in the week. Does anyone know what day this is?"

"Today!" one of the Jessicas shouted.

"Yes, it's today," replied Mrs. Greenstein in her soft, patient teacher voice. "But it has a special name, just the way you have a special name."

"My special name is Honeykins," said Jessica.

"Honeykins! That's a stupid name," said Travis.

"Travis. We don't make fun of people in this class," Mrs. Greenstein said. "Honeykins is a special name that Jenna's parents call her at home."

"I'm not Jenna. I'm Jessica," said Jessica.

"Oh, yes, of course. I'm sorry I made that mistake. You're Jessica, and that's your special name in this class," said Mrs. Greenstein.

"It's my name, too," pointed out the other Jessica.

"Yes, it is," said Mrs. Greenstein. "And the name of today is Friday. All the days in the week have names. Listen: Monday, Tuesday, Wednesday, Thursday, Friday, Saturday, Sunday."

"I know the names of the months," Marius informed his teacher.

"Really?" said Mrs. Greenstein, too surprised to become annoyed that her lesson had been interrupted.

"Yes. Listen. I'll show you.

"Thirty days hath September,
April, June, and November.
All the rest have thirty-one
Except February, which has none."

"How could a month not have any days?" asked Mrs. Greenstein. "You've got the names right, but the ending is wrong. It should be twenty-eight."

"No, I remember. February has none. My brother Lucas taught it to me. I remember."

"Lucas is not a real teacher," said Mrs. Greenstein. "So don't pay any attention to what he says. Listen to what I tell you, not to Lucas. I am the teacher."

Marius was sure that Lucas was a good teacher, but he didn't argue with Mrs. Greenstein. How could she know? She'd never seen Lucas teach. Practically everything he and Marcus knew, they'd learned from Lucas—how to tie their shoelaces, how to eat corn on the cob, how to ride their two-wheeled bikes, how to climb on the jungle gym, how to make bubbles with bubble gum, how to pump themselves on the swings, how to work the VCR and the computer, how to say "The Pledge of Allegiance." Everything.

Soon it was time to get ready to go home. Mrs. Greenstein went to her desk and brought back a pile of papers. "These are notes for you to give to your parents," she said. "Cole, will you give one paper to each student."

They all held out their hands and grabbed the papers as Cole distributed them.

Marius looked at the white sheet in his hand. This is what it said:

Dear Parents,

In order to eliminate the concern about lost or stolen money that has arisen from time to time in the past, no child in any grade is to carry more than $1.00 at any time.

The parents of those children who are buying lunch in the school cafeteria are asked to bring the money directly into the school office or to mail it to the school building.

It is important that this rule be adhered to by all

children. If more money is found on a child, it will be confiscated by the teacher and returned directly to the parent.

Marius read the note. "A hundred dollars!" he shouted out. "We're not allowed to bring a hundred dollars to school."

"A hundred dollars?" asked one of the Jessicas.

"I don't have a hundred dollars," said Travis.

"Me neither!" said Jonah.

"Marius, what are you talking about?" asked Mrs. Greenstein.

"I just read what it said on the paper," Marius explained. "I was telling everyone that there's a rule that we can't bring a hundred dollars to school."

"The message says one dollar," said the teacher. "There's a decimal point after the one. But how could you read it?"

"With my eyes," Marius explained. "That's how I always read everything." He thought for a moment. "What's a decimal point?"

"You mean you know how to read this message?" asked Mrs. Greenstein, holding up a copy of the paper that Cole had distributed.

Marius nodded. He took his copy of the message and read it all out loud. There were just two words that stumped him. They were the words *adhered* and *confiscated*.

"Amazing," said Mrs. Greenstein. "I had no idea that you knew how to read."

"You never asked me," said Marius. "I can read all the books in the library corner. My brother Lucas taught me. He taught me a long time ago."

"Can your brother Marcus read, too?" asked the teacher.

"Sure," said Marius. "Lucas used to play school with us, and he taught us both."

"Amazing," said Mrs. Greenstein again.

"Should I give myself a pat on the back?" asked Marius.

"Why, I guess you should," said the teacher. "And I guess you'd better give one to Lucas when you get home."

"I will," said Marius. "And I'll give Marcus one, too," he added. He wondered what his brother was doing across the hall.

"Fine," said Mrs. Greenstein.

The first week of kindergarten was over. As Marius marched out the door with his class-mates, he proudly patted himself on the back.

"Is It Time for School?"

Two weeks into the school year, Marcus and Marius were still waking up earlier and earlier each day. One morning it was only a quarter to six when the boys came into their parents' bedroom. They were eager to eat breakfast and get off to school. Marcus began clapping his hands just like Ms. Boscobel: *CLAP, CLAP, clap-clap-clap*. Whenever she did it, everyone knew to pay attention.

Marcus repeated the claps a second time. Still his parents lay sleeping under their blankets. "It always works for Ms. Boscobel," he said. Marius shrugged, and the boys shook their mother until she was awake.

Mrs. Cott looked sleepily at her sons and then at the clock near the bed. "We don't have to leave the house for over *two* hours," she whispered. "Go back to sleep."

A moaning sound came from the other side of the bed. It was Mr. Cott, who had pulled the covers over his head.

"I'm all awake," said Marius. "I'm ready to get ready for school."

He hadn't known he was going to enjoy kindergarten so much. But now that he'd spent so many days in Mrs. Greenstein's classroom, he liked being at school better than staying home.

"Me too. Me too," Marcus agreed. He was in a big hurry to see what Ms. Boscobel had planned for her class today.

"Then go play quietly in your bedroom," said their mother as she buried her head in her pillow. "Only babies wake their mothers this early in the morning."

The boys ran off to their bedroom, and they passed the time by building a castle using the wooden blocks that had once belonged to their big brother, Lucas. All was quiet until they decided to play crash-the-castle, and all the blocks came tumbling down.

The next morning they again woke their parents. "Is it time to get ready for school?" Marcus shouted impatiently in his mother's ear. "Is it time to get ready?"

Mrs. Cott turned her head and opened her eyes with difficulty. The light from the clock showed the time: 5:31.

"No," she whispered. "It's not time."

Mr. Cott sat up in bed. "Listen, you guys," he said as he stretched his arms over his head. "I have big plans for the weekend."

"Are we going to the zoo?" shrieked Marcus with delight. "Are we going to the zoo?"

"No," said his father, shaking his head.

"The aquarium!" shouted Marius. "I like the aquarium better than the zoo. I like the sharks."

"Me too," agreed Marcus eagerly. "I like sharks, too. And eels."

"Nope," said Mr. Cott. "No sharks, no eels, no aquarium."

"The movies?" asked Marcus. "What movie are we going to see?"

"No movie. No trip at all. We're going to stay

home and learn something very important."

"What?" asked both brothers in unison.

"You're going to learn how to tell time. And I'm going to buy a big clock to put in your bedroom so you'll know when you should get up in the morning."

"I get up when I'm finished sleeping," said Marius.

"Fair enough," said his father. "But that doesn't mean you have to wake your mother and me. We're not finished sleeping."

Mrs. Cott pulled herself up in bed. She turned to her husband and said sleepily, "Believe it or not, we're really very lucky."

"Lucky?" asked Mr. Cott. "Lucky to be wakened at this ridiculous hour?"

"Some kids hate school," said Mrs. Cott, covering her mouth as she yawned. "There were at least three children crying in the kindergarten rooms yesterday morning. They all wanted to go home."

"I don't hate school. I love it," said Marius. He thought of the planned trip to the fire station. Mrs. Greenstein said they would even get a chance to sit in the fire truck. He'd always wanted to do that!

"I love school, too," bragged Marcus. He thought happily of the huge dinosaur his class was constructing out of cardboard boxes. When they finished, it was going to be as tall as the ceiling. "I don't cry at school, and I don't throw up. Eudora throws up every day. Every day!"

"Maybe she's sick," said Mr. Cott, getting out of bed. "Her mother should take her to see a doctor."

"She did," said Marcus. "Eudora's mother told Ms. Boscobel that the doctor said she wasn't sick at all."

"Poor Eudora," said Mrs. Cott.

"Poor King George," said Marcus. "Poor King George. He has to come and clean up our classroom every day."

"Poor Ms. Boscobel," said Mrs. Cott.

"Poor me," said Marcus. "My classroom smells of throw up." He thought for a moment. "But I don't care. I'm getting used to it."

"My classroom smells of mice!" shouted Marius. "It's better than your class."

"But you didn't see any mice," Marcus reminded his brother. "You didn't see a single one."

41

"No, but I smell them. I'm lucky to be in the mouse room."

"I'm lucky to be in Ms. Boscobel's class," said Marcus. "We're always doing neat things in our class. Ms. Boscobel has the best ideas of things to do."

"I'm lucky to be in Mrs. Greenstein's class," said Marius. "We're going to make things and go on special trips, too."

"Your teacher's name sounds like Mrs. Greenbean," noted Marcus. "Ms. Boscobel is a better name for a teacher."

"Mrs. Greenstein is a perfect name for a teacher," Marius insisted.

"You boys are both fortunate. Both of your teachers are wonderful," said Mrs. Cott.

Marcus climbed up onto his parents' bed. "Ms. Boscobel is going to teach us cooking. We're going to make peanut butter next week."

"Pooh," said Marius, also climbing up onto the bed. "My class is going to make applesauce. We're going to put red-hot cinnamon candies in it to make the applesauce *red*."

The two boys argued back and forth until breakfast time. Each one remained convinced that he was in the best kindergarten class with the best teacher.

Finally, though, they were dressed and sitting at the table for the morning meal. Marius asked for a piece of cheese.

"Cheese?" asked Mrs. Cott. She was delighted with this request. Marius hadn't eaten any cheese—not American, Swiss, or even cream cheese—since he had developed a preference for red food.

Mrs. Cott put a package of orange-colored American cheese on the table. Lucas took a slice and chewed it into the shape of a mustache. "Hey, you guys, look at me," he said as he stuck the piece of cheese under his nose.

"I can do that. I can do that!" Marcus crowed with delight as he pressed some cheese under his nose, too.

"Lucas. You're supposed to set a good example for your brothers," scolded Mr. Cott, who today was eating breakfast with his family instead of leaving early in the morning as he usually did. Despite his scolding, he started laughing at the sight of the two orange mustaches on his sons.

Mrs. Cott didn't laugh. "Shave those off and into your mouths," she said. "Lucas. Sometimes I wonder if you're ever going to grow up."

"*I* didn't make a mustache," said Marius

smugly. He was glad no one had noticed that he had slipped his piece of cheese into his pocket. He was planning to break it into bits and put it around his classroom for the mouse, or mice, in the walls. He had already done that on several occasions with the snack-time crackers. But after all this time, there had been no results. Everyone knew that what mice really liked was cheese.

He was eager for the mouse to show up in class. That would prove to Marcus, once and for all, that Mrs. Greenstein's class was the best.

Ms. Boscobel's Class

When Marcus entered his class later that morning, he joined two classmates who were building with blocks on the floor. Though he thought it would be better if his twin was with him, Marcus was adjusting well to their separation.

Suddenly, the door to the room opened and in walked Lucas's friend Julio. Marcus was so delighted to recognize Julio that he jumped up to greet him and accidentally knocked over the parking garage that he and Jordan and Sam had been building.

"Look what you did," shouted Jordan angrily.

"Yeah," Sam cried out. "You meanie. You ruined all our hard work." Tears began to run down Sam's cheeks.

Marcus ignored them and rushed over toward Julio.

"Julio," he shouted, grabbing the arm of Lucas's classmate. He wanted everyone to see that this big boy who had come into their class was someone he knew. "Julio."

"Hi, Marius." Julio greeted him with a big smile.

Marcus frowned. He'd forgotten that Julio always confused him with his brother.

Luckily, Julio noticed the expression on Marcus's face and quickly corrected himself. "I mean Marcus," Julio said. "I'm going to be a mentor in your class."

"What's that?" asked Marcus. He remembered that Lucas had been talking about mentors just last night, but he forgot what it was. "What's that?"

"It's sort of like being a teacher."

Marcus nodded his head. He remembered now. He had been disappointed, because Lucas said he was going to be a mentor in one of the afternoon classes, not the morning ones.

Ms. Boscobel clapped her hands for attention. She did it her special way. *CLAP, CLAP, clap-clap-clap.* Whenever she did it, everyone was to stop what they were doing and clap their hands together, too. *CLAP, CLAP, clap-clap-clap.* "Come and sit on the rug area," Ms. Boscobel said. "I have an announcement to make."

Marcus let go of Julio's arm and rushed to sit on the front edge of the carpet, closest to his teacher's chair.

Julio sat down on the rug next to Marcus, who grinned. Lucas had many friends, but Julio was the one that Marcus liked best.

When everyone was seated, Ms. Boscobel asked Julio to stand up. "This is Julio Sanchez," she informed her students. "He is in sixth grade, and he is going to be visiting our class for an hour each week."

"He's a mentor," Marcus shouted out, proud to know the word.

"That's right," said Ms. Boscobel. "Mrs. Checchia, one of the sixth-grade teachers, has arranged that over the course of the school year each of her students will have a turn spending some time in a kindergarten class. So Julio will be here to help me and help you. Some days he'll read to you. Other times he may help you if we are doing a craft or a cooking project."

"My brother Lucas is in Mrs. Checchia's class," Marcus announced. "And Julio is my friend," he added. It wasn't exactly true. Julio was Lucas's friend, but it almost counted.

"We're going to review our colors this morning," said Ms. Boscobel, ignoring Marcus. "I have some cards with different colors. Julio is going to hold them up, and you can raise your hand if you know the color."

Ms. Boscobel got up from her chair and gestured for Julio to take her seat. Then she walked over to the closet and removed a large envelope. "Here are the cards," she said to Julio. "Hold them up. One at a time." She moved away.

"Pay attention to Julio," she told her students. "For a little while, he's going to be the teacher."

Marcus looked at Julio with admiration. Someday, he would be just as big as Julio and Lucas, and he would be a mentor, too.

Even before Julio could start teaching, Kimberly called out, "Julio. Look! I have a loose tooth." She wiggled it to show Julio. She had already shown it to Ms. Boscobel and all of her classmates.

"My brother has a loose tooth," Paul announced.

"I have a loose tongue!" Marcus called out. He stuck his tongue out and wiggled it about in his mouth.

"I can do that, too," said Jordan.

Instantly, all the kindergarten students stuck their tongues out at Julio and wiggled them about.

"I have a loose head," shouted Marcus. He began twisting his head back and forth. At once all his classmates did the same.

"My arms are loose," Marcus shouted. He began waving his arms in the air. Everyone else copied his action. Marcus was surprised at how easy it was to lead his class. In fact, maybe he was even better at it than Julio!

Julio looked over toward Ms. Boscobel. "What am I supposed to do now?" he asked helplessly.

"Go on. Pull a card out of the envelope," Ms. Boscobel called to him.

Julio stuck his hand into the envelope and pulled out a large card. "What color is this?" he asked the kindergarten children.

"Mashed potatoes!" shouted Marcus before anyone else could answer.

Julio smiled. "Yep," he said. "It's the same color as mashed potatoes. What color is that?"

The children looked at one another.

"Vanilla ice cream," said Sam. He'd been picking his nose, and he stopped for a moment to give his response.

"Yep." Julio nodded his head and looked at Ms. Boscobel again for help.

"Tell Julio what color mashed potatoes and vanilla ice cream are," Ms. Boscobel called from the side of the room where she was standing.

"It's no color at all," said Eudora.

"It *is* a color," said Ms. Boscobel. "It's white. The color white." She looked at Julio. "Try a different card," she suggested.

Julio put his hand into the envelope and pulled out another card. "What's this?" he asked, waving it in the air.

"Orange," Marcus and several of his classmates called out at the same time.

"Right," said Julio.

"Remember what I've been teaching you about raising your hand?" called out Ms. Boscobel.

Marcus raised his hand.

"What is it?" asked Julio.

"Orange," said Marcus. "It's orange."

"Yep," said Julio.

"Ask them if they know anything that is that color," Ms. Boscobel instructed her new assistant.

"Do you know anything that is this color?" asked Julio.

"Oranges," suggested Jordan.

Marcus remembered to raise his hand. "Orange juice," he said when Julio called on him. "Orange juice."

"Anything else?" asked Julio, looking around at the other students.

Amy raised her hand. "Jack-o'-lanterns," she said. She pointed to a picture of a carved pumpkin that was on the wall in anticipation of Halloween.

"Good," said Julio. He reached into the envelope and pulled out the next card.

"Green," all the children called out.

"You're supposed to raise your hand," Julio reminded them.

Eudora raised her hand. "Green," she said when Julio called on her.

"Do you know anything that is green?" asked Julio.

Paul raised his hand. "Grass," he said.

"Good," said Julio. "Anything else?"

"Green beans," said Kimberly.

"My brother Marius is in Mrs. Greenbean's class," said Marcus. "My brother is in Mrs. Greenbean's class."

"Greenstein, not Greenbean," said Julio.

"It's almost the same," said Marcus.

"No, it's not," said Julio.

"Yes, it is. Yes, it is," Marcus insisted.

"Can you think of anything else that's green?" Julio called out, trying to ignore Marcus.

"Spinach."

"Broccoli."

"Zucchini."

"I've got a zucchini bathing suit," said Kimberly.

"What's a zucchini bathing suit?" asked Julio, looking confused. "Is it green?"

Kimberly shook her head. "It's a different color. Not green."

"Bikini," Ms. Boscobel called out from the side of the room. "She's got a *bikini* bathing suit."

"You should raise your hand," Marcus

reminded her. "If Julio is the teacher, then you have to be just like us. You have to raise your hand, too."

Julio laughed aloud and pulled out another card. "What's this?" he asked, trying to look serious.

Marcus raised his hand. "Tomato sauce," he said, eliminating the name of the color and once again going directly to the food it represented.

"What color is it?" asked Julio.

"Red," said Paul.

"It's the same color as the stuff coming out of Sam's nose," said Jordan.

Everyone turned to look at Sam. Sure enough, some red was dripping down from his nose.

"That's blood," shrieked Amy. "He's bleeding."

Half the children jumped up to get a closer look. The other half of the group kept their distance. Ms. Boscobel came running across the room. "It's just a simple nosebleed," she shouted. "It's nothing to get excited about." Marcus thought she sounded very excited.

"I'm not excited," he said. "It's not my nose."

"There's blood on the floor!" Amy shouted. "Sam got blood on the floor."

"Julio. Watch the students," said Ms. Boscobel. "I'm taking Sam to the nurse's office."

"I'm not sick," Sam cried out as Ms. Boscobel rushed him out of the room. "I don't want to go to a nurse."

Julio let out a long sigh. "Everybody sit down," he said.

"My nose isn't bleeding. Is your nose bleeding?" Jordan asked Paul.

"My nose was bleeding once. But then it stopped," said Kevin.

"Everybody sit down," shouted Julio in a loud voice.

"Don't sit by the blood!" warned Eudora.

Julio looked around at the little kids. "What do you usually do now?" he asked Marcus.

"We play games," Marcus announced. "Remember how once you played Simon Says with Marius and me? We could play that now." He rushed to stand next to Julio. "I'll help you," he said.

"Okay," Julio agreed, relieved to have a plan of action.

By the time Ms. Boscobel and Sam returned to the room, all of the students were silently tapping their heads. Sam's nose was no longer bleeding, and he was licking a lollipop. It was the same color as broccoli, spinach, zucchini, and grass.

"I stopped doing the colors," said Julio. "I think they did enough for one day."

"That's fine," said Ms. Boscobel. "And I see you were playing a game with them. That's fine, too. You are a natural teacher, Julio. You knew just what to do with the children to keep their attention. Maybe you'll get a job as a teacher when you grow up."

"Oh, no," said Julio, jumping out of Ms. Boscobel's chair. "This is too hard. I never knew it was so hard to be a teacher. I'm going back to my class. Mrs. Checchia is going to give us a math quiz in a little while. That's going to be a cinch after this."

"Good-bye, Julio," Marcus called as Julio walked toward the door.

"Good-bye," all the other children echoed.

Marcus couldn't wait to tell Lucas all about

Julio's visit to his class. He wondered who was the mentor in Marius's classroom. Whoever it was, it wouldn't be as good as having their friend Julio. Poor Marius had to be in the other kindergarten. Marcus was in the best kindergarten class of all.

Back inside the Teachers' Room

Ms. Boscobel came into the teachers' room and plopped down onto a chair. She let out a loud sigh. It had been another hard morning, and she was exhausted. She opened her tote bag and pulled out a paper bag. She put her hand into the bag and took out a sugared donut.

"Are you really going to eat that?" asked Mrs. Greenstein. "I thought you were on a diet."

"Diets are not for people who teach kindergarten in this school. Especially people who have Marcus Cott in their class." Ms. Boscobel sighed. "All morning I kept thinking about this donut. I told myself that when I was sitting and eating it at lunchtime, the worst of the day would be over. And today is Thursday. That means the worst of the week is over as well. Just one more day, and then we have the weekend to look forward to."

"I know how you feel," said Mrs. Greenstein. She looked at the carrot sticks spread out on a piece of waxed paper in front of her. "I wish I had a donut myself."

Ms. Boscobel smiled and handed over her paper bag. Inside was a second donut.

"What a treat!" Mrs. Greenstein said as she took a large bite. "Thank you," she said through a mouthful of donut. As usual, the two kinder-garten teachers were alone in the room. Their classes were dismissed fifteen minutes before any of the other grades had lunch. They always had those fifteen minutes together before they were joined by other teachers.

"So tell me. What did darling Marcus do today?"

"Listen to this," began Ms. Boscobel. "The tops of the windows in my classroom were open this morning, and a small bird flew into the room. Some of the children were very upset—after all, they've never seen a bird flying around inside the classroom before. The bird couldn't find its way out, and it flew from one corner of the room to the other as the kids screamed and shouted."

"I did hear screams coming from your room," said Mrs. Greenstein. "I wondered what was going on."

"Well, Marcus climbed up on one of the tables and tried to catch the bird. Naturally, several of the other kids climbed up on the table, too. I had to get all of them down before someone fell. At the same time, I had to calm the children who were frightened."

"What happened next?" asked Mrs. Greenstein.

"Then Marcus led everyone in shouting instructions to the bird, like 'Fly out the window.' He also had advice for me, like 'Open the windows' and 'Open the doors.' But the windows were already open, and it would make no sense to have the bird flying helplessly in the hallway. So I told two of the girls to see if they could find Mr. King. I thought he might know what to do."

"And did he?"

"Well, yes, eventually. But before he came, Marcus had half the children running around the room, flapping their arms like birds. And then the very worst thing happened."

"Mr. Herbertson walked into your room?" gasped Mrs. Greenstein.

"Oh, no. Thank goodness for that," said Ms. Boscobel. "But it was still something awful. The poor bird crashed into one of the glass windowpanes and dropped to the floor."

"Was it dead?"

"We all thought so. Two children began crying. The others rushed over to investigate. Sam Fenton said he thought we should all say a prayer. Well, since we're not supposed to pray together in school, I wasn't sure what to do next. Luckily, just then the two girls returned with Mr. King."

"That's good," said Mrs. Greenstein, licking the sugar off her fingers.

"No, it was bad, because Mr. King picked up the bird and suddenly it began to move. The children thought it was the bird's ghost, and of course everyone screamed louder than ever. But then Marcus shouted out, 'King George, you brought him back to life. You're magic!' So Mr.

King put the little bird on a branch of one of the trees out in the yard. We watched from the window and saw it fly away."

"What a nice ending," observed Mrs. Greenstein. "You got off very easy having Marcus in your class," she commented. "Take it from me, you don't know what a difficult student is like."

"There is no way that Marius is as difficult as Marcus," insisted Ms. Boscobel.

"Oh no? Well, listen to this," said Mrs. Greenstein. "Remember Cecelia Griffin's mother, who came to school on Tuesday to talk about being an author?"

"Of course," responded Ms. Boscobel.

"Well, after she spoke to our classes, I asked her to autograph the copy of her book that we had in our room. And this morning, our sixth-grade mentor, Cricket Kaufman, discovered Marius scribbling with a pen inside all the books in our library corner. First she let out a shriek of horror. Then when I rushed over to see what the problem was, I heard her demanding to know what he thought he was doing. He said he was playing that he was an author."

Ms. Boscobel giggled. "That's really funny," she said. "No wonder he did that. We always tell

children not to write in books and then we make a big deal about asking an author to do exactly that."

"Go ahead and laugh," said Mrs. Greenstein. "The books in your classroom aren't all marked up with ink scribbles. I don't know who was more upset, me or poor Cricket. I thought she was going to start crying. She said, 'He should be arrested for doing that.'"

"Well, I don't care what you say," said Ms. Boscobel. "I still feel that Marcus is much more difficult than Marius."

"He certainly is not," said her colleague as the door to the teachers' room opened and several faculty members came inside.

"This school year is never going to end." Ms. Boscobel sighed.

"Sounds like you have a tough class this year," commented a third-grade teacher, Mrs. Hockaday, who had just entered the room with several other teachers.

Ms. Boscobel nodded her head. "Actually, the whole class isn't so bad. It's just one who seems to set everyone else off."

"Well, you know what they say about rotten apples," commented another teacher. "It only takes one to spoil all the others in the barrel."

Two third-grade boys, who had been walking down the hallway outside, stuck their heads through the open door of the teachers' room. All the children in the school were fascinated by the room, which was off-limits to them. Mrs. Hockaday got up from her chair and closed the door.

"Lillian has Marius Cott. And I have his twin brother, Marcus," Ms. Boscobel explained. "But I'm certain that Marcus is much more of a problem than Marius," she added.

"I had their older brother, Lucas, when he was in third grade," said Mrs. Hockaday, nodding her head. "But you know, in the end, he wasn't so bad."

"Well, Marcus isn't bad. He's awful," said Ms. Boscobel.

"Marius is worse," asserted Mrs. Greenstein. "Much worse."

Mrs. Forrest, a second-grade teacher who was standing near the microwave oven, looked over at the two kindergarten teachers. "What the two of you should do is trade classes for a morning. Then you'd know who has the more difficult student."

Ms. Boscobel looked at Mrs. Greenstein. "That's not such a bad idea," she said. "I could use an easy morning for once."

"Easy? One morning in my classroom and you'd know what hard work really is," said Mrs. Greenstein.

"Pick a day," suggested Ms. Boscobel. "I'd love to switch with you. Even for an hour."

"All right," agreed Mrs. Greenstein. "How about Monday morning? We'll tell the students that I have to do some sort of work in your classroom. It shouldn't be difficult to arrange."

Ms. Boscobel held her hand out across the lunch table. "It's a deal," she said. "And I'll even bring a bag of donuts again on Monday. You'll need something to look forward to when the morning is over."

"I can't wait to hear how this turns out," said Mrs. Forrest. "Bring me a donut, too. It was my idea."

Mrs. Greenstein gathered her things together. It was time to get ready for her afternoon class.

"I'm looking forward to our exchange," she told Ms. Boscobel.

"Me too," said the younger teacher. "For

once I won't be dreading Monday morning. In fact, I'll be looking forward to it."

"Just don't forget the donuts," Mrs. Greenstein reminded the other kindergarten teacher. "You're going to need them."

"So will you. You'll see."

Trading Places

It was the first Monday in October. School had been in session for four weeks. In the two sections of morning kindergarten, the pattern of the day was set. The teachers and the children had mastered everyone's names. Students in Mrs. Greenstein's class knew that giving oneself a pat on the back was a big honor. Students in Ms. Boscobel's class knew that the thing that seemed to bother her the most was a drippy nose. "Take a tissue and blow," she always said, pointing to the box on her desk. In both classes,

69

Friday was "color" day, when the children came to school wearing clothing that was the color of the week. Last Friday it had been blue.

On Monday, both Mrs. Greenstein and Ms. Boscobel came into the school building smiling and eager to start the new week. They each stopped in their own room to leave their jackets and pocketbooks in the closets. Then they walked out of their rooms and met in the hall. "I was going to review the alphabet this morning," said Mrs. Greenstein. "But feel free to do anything you want."

"Have you read this?" asked Ms. Boscobel. She held up a copy of *Harry the Dirty Dog*.

"No. I don't have that book in my room," said Mrs. Greenstein.

"It's an old favorite of mine," said Ms. Boscobel. "I read it aloud last week and my children loved it. I'll read it to your group this morning."

"Fine," agreed the other kindergarten teacher. "Have fun. And if Marius drives you crazy, remember you'll be able to escape back to your own room before long."

Ms. Boscobel laughed. "You're the one who's going to come running," she predicted.

Now, it just so happened that on their way to

school that morning, Marcus and Marius began to protest that their mother walked with them every morning. Now that they were no longer in preschool, they weren't babies. They knew the way to school. Why couldn't they walk to school alone like the other kids they saw along their route?

"Can't we go by ourselves?" Marius begged his mother.

"Next year, maybe," said Mrs. Cott.

"Next year? That's a hundred years from now," complained Marcus. "A hundred years."

"I have an idea," suggested Mrs. Cott. "I'll walk you to the corner of the street with the school. Then you two can walk the last half block·by yourselves."

"Yippee," shouted Marcus. "That's almost like walking all the way alone."

"No, it's not," said Marius.

But Mrs. Cott would not budge. "I'm going to walk you to the last corner and that's that," she insisted.

So Marius had to be satisfied with pretending that he'd walked all the way to school like a big kid, even though he'd only done it for the last little bit.

Then Marius got a great idea. After their

mother left the boys at the corner, he said to his brother, "Let's go say hi to Lucas before we go inside the school."

Their mother had taken them once to see Lucas at his Safety Patrol post. Both boys had been impressed by the way that Lucas stood waving his hand to instruct the students when to cross the street. They had both decided that they wanted to wear a sash and a badge and be on the Safety Patrol as soon as they were in sixth grade.

"Do you know which way it is to where Lucas stands?" asked Marcus.

"Sure," said Marius.

The twins walked past the school's entrance and past all the children getting off of buses and hanging around in front of the building.

"It's down this next street," said Marius, hoping he was right. He looked around for some sort of landmark, but the houses on the street looked very much like all the others in the area.

"Okay," agreed Marcus, jumping along. He had discovered that if he held his two feet together and jumped, he could cover as much ground as if he walked normally.

"Do you remember the name of the street?"

Marius asked Marcus. They had reached a crossing area, but another boy—not their brother—was on duty here.

"Nope."

Boys and girls streamed past them in the opposite direction, toward the school.

"I think it's down the next street," said Marius hopefully.

Marcus called out to a girl wearing the blue sash and silver badge of a Safety Patrol member. "Do you know Lucas Cott? He's our brother."

"Sure, I know him," the girl said.

"Which way is his street?" asked Marius.

"I don't know what post he's got," the girl replied. "Besides, it's time to go to school. You'd better come with me."

"No way, José," shouted Marius, and he started running off.

Marcus followed his brother. "Why are we running?" he called to Marius.

"We don't want to walk to school with that girl," he told Marcus.

They turned around, but the girl wasn't following them.

"You know what?" Marcus asked Marius.

"No. What?" said Marius.

"We're lost. I don't remember which way the school is."

"It's back down that way," said Marius, pointing, but Marcus wasn't sure.

The two boys walked in the direction that Marius had picked. Marcus hoped they were going the right way.

"Do you think we'll ever find our way back again?" Marcus asked. It had been fun looking for Lucas. But now he wanted to be sitting in his class. He would have liked listening to Ms. Boscobel read a story or singing with his classmates. Maybe it would be snack time. Marcus would have liked a few crackers and a glass of juice.

"I'm tired," said Marcus. He sat down in the middle of the sidewalk. "I don't want to walk any more. Lucas is at school by now. We'll never find him."

"Who's that coming this way?" asked Marius. He pointed to a boy a block off who was running in their direction.

"It looks a little like...," Marcus began.

"Lucas!" shouted both twins in unison. They ran to greet their brother.

"What in the world are you doing here?" Lucas demanded.

"What are *you* doing here?" Marius questioned back.

"I came looking for you," said Lucas. "One of the girls in the Safety Patrol told me she saw you walking in the wrong direction."

"We were looking for you," said Marcus.

"We didn't know it was the wrong direction," Marius explained.

"Well, we better get going to school," said Lucas. "We're all late."

"I'm tired," Marcus complained. "I'm tired of walking."

"That's because you weren't walking. You were jumping," Marius pointed out.

"I don't care. I don't feel like walking to school." Marcus sat down again on the sidewalk.

"We can't leave him," said Marius. He sat down on the sidewalk next to Marcus.

"Look, you guys," said Lucas helplessly. "There's no bus that goes this way. And you're too big for me to carry you. So you have to walk. That's all there is to it. Get up and start walking."

"No," said Marcus, shaking his head.

"I don't want to," said Marius.

The twins remained sitting on the sidewalk.

Lucas sat down beside them on the curb.

"Listen," he said. "It's not a big deal to miss kindergarten. But sixth grade is important. I'm missing a spelling quiz right this minute. You guys are getting me in big, big trouble."

"Really?" asked Marcus.

"Really," said Lucas. He stood up. "So I guess I'm going to have to leave you both here and go by myself."

"Really?" asked Marius.

"Really," said Lucas, taking a couple of small steps in the direction of the school. "Good-bye," he called to the twins. Lucas took another couple of steps.

"Wait!" shouted Marcus. "Wait."

"We're coming," Marius called out.

There was no one outside the building to notice their late arrival. "Now we have to go to the office and get late passes," Lucas explained to his brothers.

"What's a late pass?" asked Marcus. "What's a late pass?"

"You can't get into your class without it if you don't get to school on time," Lucas explained as he led his brothers toward the office.

"Uh-oh. Are we going to get in trouble?" asked Marius.

"Probably," said Lucas.

"What will happen?" asked Marcus.

Lucas shrugged. He was an old hand at getting in trouble. His career as a class clown had started back when he was Marcus and Marius's age. But in the last couple of years he'd begun shaping up.

"Look. If you really and truly promise me that you'll always come straight into school and not go looking for me or wandering off, I'll cover for you this time," Lucas offered.

"I promise," said Marius. "I don't want to get in trouble."

"Me too," said Marcus. "I don't want to get in trouble, either. I don't want to make Ms. Boscobel angry at me."

Lucas entered the office holding his brothers by the hand. "Wait here," he said, letting go of their hands and pointing to a bench along one wall in the office.

As their brother spoke to the school secretary, the twins spoke together in hushed voices.

"Mrs. Greenstein won't get angry that I'm late," said Marius. "She never yells. Even when she doesn't like what I'm doing she says, 'Marius. I told you not to behave that way,' but she says it in a nice voice."

"Ms. Boscobel won't yell, either," said Marcus. "She loves me and I love her. She's a perfect teacher. She's better than Mrs. Greenbean."

"Stop calling her that," said Marius angrily. "She's Mrs. Greenstein, and she's the best teacher in the whole school."

"No, she's not. The best teacher is Ms. Boscobel," Marcus insisted.

"Mine's the best," said Marius. "Mrs. Greenstein knows about everything: dinosaurs, birds, planets, how to make things out of paper, and cooking the best foods, and, and, and..." He stopped to catch his breath.

"No. Me. I'm the lucky one," Marcus insisted. "Ms. Boscobel knows everything your teacher knows, and she smells good, too. She smells like flowers."

"It would be better if she smelled like chocolate," Marius responded. "If you came to my class, you'd see it's better than yours," he told his brother.

"I don't believe you," Marcus responded. He

thought for a moment. "Do you think Mrs. Greenstein is worrying about where you are right now?" he asked. "I know Ms. Boscobel is very lonely for me."

"I know Mrs. Greenstein is very sad that I'm not at school," Marius said. "If you were in my class, you'd see I'm right."

And that's how the idea came to him. He leaned over to Marcus and whispered a plan.

"Is everything all right now?" the secretary asked the twins when she finished speaking to Lucas.

"Yep. Everything's fine," Lucas answered for them.

The secretary gave each of the boys a piece of paper. "Present this to your teachers," she told them.

The three boys went out into the hallway. "Okay. Go off to your classrooms right now. I'll see you this afternoon," Lucas said. He watched as Marcus and Marius headed toward the kindergarten rooms.

The twins smiled at each other as they walked. No one had ever told the boys that they couldn't pretend to be each other. And people confused their identities all the time. So what would be wrong if one morning Marius pretended to be Marcus, while Marcus pretended to be Marius? That way they would know once and for all which was the best kindergarten teacher and which was the best kindergarten class.

·8·

Who's Who?

Marius ran toward Ms. Boscobel's class-room. To his surprise, instead of Ms. Boscobel, he found his own teacher, Mrs. Greenstein, in the room.

"What are *you* doing here?" he demanded to know.

"Good morning, Marcus," Mrs. Greenstein greeted him, taking the late pass out of his hand. She didn't know the names of all the other students in her colleague's class, but there was no difficulty in recognizing Marius's brother.

"I'm glad to see you made it. I was beginning to think you were absent today."

"No, I'm here," Marius said. "But why are you here?"

"Ms. Boscobel and I are spending a little time in each other's classrooms this morning," the teacher explained. "Now, why don't you go hang up your backpack in your cubby and sit on the rug?" Marius wrinkled his nose as he walked into the classroom. How was he going to find out about Ms. Boscobel if Mrs. Greenstein was here in her place? He'd better go back to his regular kindergarten. That's where he'd find Ms. Boscobel.

Marius turned around and started out the door. But Mrs. Greenstein caught him by the sleeve. "Didn't you hear what I told you?" she said.

"Yeah," Marius agreed. "But I belong in the other classroom."

"Marcus," said Mrs. Greenstein in a slow, calm voice. "I know it seems strange to you that your regular teacher isn't here this morning. But I promise you, she'll be back before you know it. In the meantime, I want you to sit down with all your classmates and not to worry about who is teaching your class."

"I'm not Marcus," Marius said. "So I should go to the other room."

"Marcus," said Mrs. Greenstein, her voice rising ever so slightly. "I know perfectly well that you are not Marius. Don't forget that Marius has been in my class for a full month."

"But I *am* Marius," protested Marius.

"Marcus," said Mrs. Greenstein. By now her voice was decidedly louder. "Go and sit down. Now."

"Come on, Marcus," said Jordan. "Sit next to me."

"I'm not Marcus," Marius said to his brother's classmate. "Can't you tell that I'm Marius?"

"Of course not," said Jordan. "I can't tell who you are. I just know that if you're in my class, you're Marcus. That's the same shirt you wore last week."

Marius looked down at his shirt. He and his brother wore the same size and so all their clothing was exchanged between them. Then he remembered something. "Look behind my ear," he said, pushing his hair away and tugging on his right ear. "Do you see the freckle there?"

"Yep," said Jordan.

"That proves that I'm Marius. Marcus doesn't have a freckle behind his ear."

"I never looked behind your ear before. And I never looked behind your brother's ear, either," said Jordan. "Besides, it doesn't matter about freckles." The two boys sat down on the carpet.

"Hi, Marcus," Amy and Kimberly said together. Kimberly was trying to braid Amy's hair.

"He says he's Marius today," Jordan told the girls.

"That's a good game," Amy said. "I'll be Kimberly today," she announced.

"And I'm Amy," shouted Kimberly. "I like this game."

Marius was going to continue arguing, but he realized that without Marcus next to him, he had no way to prove that he wasn't Marcus himself. He decided that if he couldn't get to know Ms. Boscobel, at least he could check out her classroom. He looked around. The windows were in different locations and the view from them was not the same as it was from his classroom, but otherwise, this kindergarten room looked almost identical to his room across the hall. And even though Mrs. Greenstein's room was supposed to smell like mice, he thought this room smelled the same way. He guessed there were mice hiding behind the walls of this room, too. He got up from the carpet and went to look under the radiator. He'd just about given up ever seeing a mouse in Mrs. Greenstein's room, but maybe he'd be luckier here.

"Marcus. What do you think you're doing?" Mrs. Greenstein called out.

Marius didn't bother correcting her about his name. She wouldn't have believed him anyhow. But he did tell her what he'd been doing.

"There are no mice in this room," she said in an angry voice. "I don't know why you and your brother are so obsessed with rodents, anyway. Now sit down. We're going to all sing a song together."

"I can sing from here," observed Marius.

"No, you can't," said Mrs. Greenstein. She was beginning to see why Ms. Boscobel found Marcus so difficult. At this point in the school year, she shouldn't have to argue with him about following directions. Perhaps Marcus *was* the more difficult of the twins after all, she conceded to herself.

"Mrs. Greenstein?" Marius called out. "If I sing the song, can I give myself a big pat on the back?"

Meanwhile, across the hall in Mrs. Greenstein's class, things weren't going so well either. Ms. Boscobel sat inside the room and smiled at each of the youngsters as they entered the classroom.

"I'm going to be your teacher, just for a little while this morning," she explained.

"Is Mrs. Greenstein sick?" asked one of the Jessicas.

"I saw her. She didn't look sick to me," said Eric.

"No. No. She's not sick. But she's teaching my students for a short time this morning while I'm here with you."

Ms. Boscobel looked about. She didn't see Marcus's twin brother anywhere.

"Hang up your jackets and sit on the rug," Ms. Boscobel instructed the children.

It took a few minutes, but eventually everyone was sitting down. Just at that moment, Marcus Cott walked into the room.

"Hi, Ms. Boscobel," he shouted, handing her his late pass. "What are you doing in here?"

"Good morning, Marius," Ms. Boscobel said, returning the greeting. And she explained once again the mystery of her presence in Mrs. Greenstein's classroom. "It's just for a little while, Marius," she reassured him.

"Don't you know me yet?" Marcus asked her when he heard her call him by his brother's name again. "I'm Marcus, not Marius. So I better get back to my own class. I'll see you later," he said, and he started to walk out of the room.

"No, no, come back," Ms. Boscobel called, jumping up and grabbing Marcus by his overall strap. "You must stay right here in this class, where you belong."

"But I don't belong here," Marcus protested. "I don't belong here."

"If you go running out of here, the next thing you know everyone in the class will go running out, too. That's not the way we do things in kindergarten. You know you must listen to your teacher and do what she says."

"But you're not our teacher," said Jessica.

"Yes, I am. Just for this morning," said Ms. Boscobel. She turned to Marcus. "Marius. Sit down right here and don't make a move unless I tell you."

Marcus sat down. He squirmed on the rug. "I moved," he announced.

"Marius. It's hard to believe, but you are exactly like your brother Marcus," said Ms. Boscobel with a sigh.

"I *am* my brother," said Marcus. "I'm Marcus."

"No joking around," said Ms. Boscobel sternly. She turned to a boy sitting near Marcus on the carpet. "What's your name?" she asked him.

"Cole."

Ms. Boscobel pointed to each child in turn.

"Jonah."

"Kayla."

"Jenna."

"Jessica."

"Jessica."

"Two Jessicas," said Ms. Boscobel with a smile. "That's easy to remember."

"You're not very good at remembering," called out Marcus. "You can't remember *me*."

"Marius. I don't want to hear a peep out of you."

"He's always talking," said one of the Jessicas.

"No, I'm not," said Marcus. "You don't even know me."

"Marius," said the other Jessica. "You were talking so much last week that Mrs. Greenstein said you were giving her a headache."

"Mrs. Greenbean said that?" asked Marcus. Marius hadn't told him that piece of news.

"It isn't polite to call your teacher that," said Ms. Boscobel. "You must always call your teacher *Mrs. Greenstein.*"

"Does that mean that we should call you Mrs. Greenstein if you are our teacher this morning?" asked Marcus.

"Don't be silly," said Ms. Boscobel impatiently.

"He's always silly," said Kayla.

Marcus sat on the rug and pouted. He didn't mind that Kayla had called him silly. And he didn't mind that Ms. Boscobel sounded annoyed with him. What bothered him was that he'd never be able to find out what sort of teacher Mrs. Greenstein was if she was off in his classroom while he was here in hers.

When Ms. Boscobel turned away from the children for a moment, Marcus saw his chance to escape back to his own classroom. He slid over on the carpet toward the edge, closer to the doorway.

"Ms. Boscobel. I have a boo-boo," said Kayla, holding out her hand to show the teacher.

"Let me see," said Ms. Boscobel. She looked at the finger that Kayla offered her.

Meanwhile, Marcus jumped up and raced toward the door.

"Teacher. Teacher," shouted Jenna, pulling her thumb out of her mouth so she could speak. "Marius is going out of the room."

Ms. Boscobel dropped Kayla's hand and darted toward the doorway. She returned a moment later with her hand holding Marcus tightly.

"Sit down and don't get up," she told him.

"Maybe he has to make pee-pee," said Jonah.

"He should have gone to the bathroom at home. We don't have toilet time this early," said Ms. Boscobel. But she looked at Marcus and asked him anyway. "Were you on your way to the boys' room?"

"No," said Marcus honestly.

"I didn't think so. You are not to get up,

no matter what. Do you hear me?"

Marcus nodded his head. It seemed to him that Ms. Boscobel scolded him more in this room than she did back in their own classroom. It didn't make sense to him. He wondered if Mrs. Greenstein noticed that Marius was with her across the hallway. And he wondered if she was scolding this much, too.

Ms. Boscobel held up the book she had brought with her. "Here is a new book that none of you have heard yet at school," she said.

"I heard it when you read it before," Marcus shouted out.

"That's impossible. Did your brother come home and tell you about the story?" asked Ms. Boscobel.

Marcus shook his head. "My brother doesn't know that story," he said. "But I do. I heard you read it."

"No, Marius. You are getting confused. I did not read this book to you yet. I am going to read it now."

"But—but—," Marcus protested.

"Marius. Please, button your mouth. I am going to read this book now."

Even though Marcus knew the whole story,

he kept his mouth shut as the teacher began reading. She was only on the second page when a loud bell began to sound.

"What's that?" asked Cole.

"It's a burglar alarm," said Eric.

"No. It's a school bell. Because we're in school," said one of the Jessicas.

"That's the bell for a fire drill," said Ms. Boscobel. "Everyone stand up and wait at the door. We've had a fire drill before. You should remember what to do."

The children all rushed to get in a line. Only one student remained sitting on the carpet.

"Double file. With a partner," said Ms. Boscobel. "Marius. Why aren't you in line?" she demanded, looking at Marcus.

"I'm not Marius. Besides, you told me to button my mouth, but I can't do that and talk to you at the same time," Marcus said innocently.

"Well, now I'm telling you to unbutton it, and I'm telling you to get in line!"

"But I thought you said I couldn't get up no matter what," Marcus reminded Ms. Boscobel.

"Marius, you are driving me mad!" exclaimed Ms. Boscobel. "Come here at once. Suppose the school was burning down. Would you just sit there?"

"Is the school burning down?" asked Kayla. She began crying.

"No. No. No. There's no fire. This is just pretend. It's practice," said Ms. Boscobel. She put her arms around Kayla. "Now don't be frightened," she told her. "We're going to march outside the school, just the way Mrs. Greenstein taught you to do."

"I'm scared," said Jenna. "Give me a hug, too."

"Me too," said Avery.

"I don't want no teachers hugging me," said Cole.

"Don't hug me," said Travis.

Marcus didn't say anything. He just marched out with the other students. He figured this would be the perfect chance to change places with his brother.

·9·

Back in Place

Within three minutes, all the students who attended Edison-Armstrong were assembled in the school parking lot. Marcus saw Mrs. Greenstein with the students from his class standing nearby. He left his class line and rushed to find his brother.

Marius looked very relieved when he saw Marcus. "Quick," he said.

Marcus scooted into Marius's place in line while Marius rushed to fill the spot that Marcus had left. Ms. Boscobel and Mrs. Greenstein didn't notice, because at that very moment they were having a quick conference together.

"I know it's not even a full hour, but I'm ready to go back to my own class, if you feel that way, too," Ms. Boscobel told Mrs. Greenstein.

"I think that's a very good idea," said Mrs. Greenstein. Her gray hair was in disarray.

"Ladies. Ladies. You know the rule. It's the same for teachers as it is for students. No talking during a fire drill unless there is some sort of emergency."

It was Mr. Herbertson speaking to his two kindergarten teachers.

"This was an emergency," said Mrs. Greenstein to the principal.

"Yes, it was," agreed Ms. Boscobel.

In a minute, the loud bell rang again. It was the signal for the teachers to return to the school building with their students.

Marius was surprised to discover that Mrs. Greenstein was leading his class instead of Ms. Boscobel.

"Which class do you like better?" he asked Mrs. Greenstein as they marched into the build-ing.

"Hush," said Mrs. Greenstein, putting her fingers to her lips. "No one is supposed to speak during a fire drill."

But back in the room, she gave her answer. "Marius," she whispered in his ear, "I missed you. I missed all of my students when I was in Ms. Boscobel's class."

"But..." Marius was about to say that he had been with her the whole time. But just in case he and Marcus tried the switch another day, he caught himself. "I missed you too, Mrs. Greenstein," he declared.

Marcus also felt good to be back in his own classroom. For some reason, Ms. Boscobel, the teacher that he dearly loved, was a nicer person in this room.

Ms. Boscobel looked around her classroom. The students were all involved in quiet activities. Even Marcus, who always gave her so much trouble, seemed angelic this morning. She was glad to be back in the room where she belonged.

When the morning ended and the students were dismissed, Ms. Boscobel rushed to the teachers' room. She opened the bag of donuts she had brought with her and offered them to Mrs. Greenstein. "You are an amazing woman to put up with that Marius Cott each day," she told her colleague. "I admit it. Marcus is easier to handle. Much easier."

"Well, my dear. It's kind of you to say that," Mrs. Greenstein responded, "but I don't know how you manage to retain your sanity. I could hardly make it through half an hour with Marcus. I'll take Marius over his brother any day."

"That's good," said Ms. Boscobel, biting into her donut. "Because we both have one hundred and sixty-two days until the school year ends."

"Look at the bright side," said Mrs. Greenstein. "Some schools have full-day kinder-garten programs. We only see those Cott boys half a day at a time."

"You're right," agreed Ms. Boscobel. "I was also thinking that it's already October. It's not as if we were just starting school."

"Thank goodness for small things," Mrs. Greenstein exclaimed.

"Have another donut," Ms. Boscobel offered.

As for Marcus and Marius, by the time the morning had ended both had almost forgotten the way it had begun. Marcus had green paint all over his shirt from a picture he had done at the class easel. Marius smelled of apple juice, because he had spilled some on himself during snack time.

"We'll go home and you'll both change," said Mrs. Cott when she saw the state of her twins.

"We already changed once today," said Marius. His mother thought he was referring to changing out of his pajamas when he woke up, so she didn't ask for an explanation. Besides, school was over for the day, and they all had other things to think about now.

"Can we stop and buy some donuts?" Marius asked his mother as they walked past a donut shop.

"Donuts aren't red," commented Mrs. Cott. She didn't add that they didn't contain any vitamins or nutrients either.

"I know," said Marius. "But I feel like eating something a different color today."

"Great," said his mother. "I'll fix some green beans to go with a grilled cheese sandwich for lunch. And if you eat it all, then we'll take a walk later and buy a donut for each of you. How does that sound?"

"It sounds delicious," shouted Marius. "Delicious."

"I wonder if Mrs. Greenbean eats green beans for her lunch?" commented Marcus.

"Greenstein. Her name is Greenstein," said Marius, correcting his brother. "And I bet she eats donuts."

once upon a time, what does it matter now? No one even knows whose tomb it might have been.'

'No. Indeed.'

Flora headed for the castle, her thoughts in a whirl.

Surely her instincts weren't wrong—that her brooch belonged on that tomb? And if the tomb *had* once been occupied, did that mean the skeleton she'd found belonged there? But why on earth would a Lochmore be in the tower at Castle McCrieff?

Father must *know the skeleton is in the Great Tower—I wonder if he knows the story behind it?*

The urge to find out more—to discover the truth—seized her. It was yet another incentive to face her family and confront them over their treatment of her. And then, one day—if they could only grow closer...if he would only grant her a voice—maybe she would find enough courage to ask her father the truth about the skeleton in the Great Tower.

But first things first. Lachlan had already warned her he must work this evening. Tomorrow, though, she would start her plan.

Chapter Twenty-One

The following morning Lachlan's study door burst open, startling him. Flora marched in and plonked herself on the chair opposite his.

He tried to hide it, but he felt his lips twitch anyway. Her lips pursed.

'You look very…er…*determined*, Flora.'

'I am, Lachlan. I have two requests of you.'

'Go on.'

'First, I wish to visit my family, so may I have the carriage?'

He tried not to frown but he couldn't help it. He didn't want to be apart from her, not even for one night.

'Of course you may; you don't have to ask. How long will you be gone?'

'I will return tomorrow.'

Very brisk. Very businesslike. It was almost as though she were following an agenda.

'And your second request?'

'May I come with you when you go to Glasgow on Monday?'

He'd had every intention of begging her to come anyway. 'Yes, of course you may. Is there a particular reason?'

Her eyes glinted. 'Apart from wanting to spend time with my husband, you mean?'

They shared a smile, easing the aching knot that had lodged in his chest ever since Anna and Davy left. He was still sad they were not here where he could look after them, but now he could view events at a distance he recognised Flora had been right. In his eagerness to make amends he had pushed Anna too hard and had failed to give any credence to her views. But understanding that didn't make their absence any less painful. They had parted on uneasy terms and he hadn't visited them since the day they moved into their new home, unsure of his welcome.

Which left Flora.

He loved her. So much. But that scared him…*petrified* him. How could he bear it if he lost her? And that fear made him cautious. And that caution, he knew, made Flora unhappy and yet all he really wanted was to make her happy.

Why could he never find the words to tell her how much she meant to him?

'Well, as you put it like that, would you…?' He hesitated. Would it be an intrusion? But he didn't like to think of her setting out on that long journey—or facing her tyrant of a father—alone. 'Would you like me to come with you?'

'Can you spare the time?'

He smiled ruefully. 'I neglected you for business last night. I think it's only fair I occasionally neglect business for my beautiful wife. Don't you?'

Her smile lit her face. He'd been right to offer. That knot eased a little more.

'Thank you, Lachlan. I would appreciate your company.'

'May I ask…is there a purpose to this visit?'

Flora straightened. 'There is. They are my family and I love them—even after the Galkirk business. I no longer feel guilty. I no longer feel I need their forgiveness, but I *do* hope they will be part of our lives in the future. If I do not make the first move, I fear that will never happen. Do you object?'

'No. Of course I don't object.'

But if any one of her family upset her he silently vowed to whisk her away from them immediately, family or no family. He would do anything to protect her.

They reached Castle McCrieff at nightfall after an arduous journey over wet, muddy roads. Flora's mother burst into tears as soon as she saw Flora, hurrying to her with hands outstretched.

'You didna warn us you were coming! Oh! I am so happy to see you, Flora.' She framed Flora's face, kissed her and hugged her tight.

Flora's eyes and mouth rounded in astonishment before she blanked her expression and stepped back, her chin jutting out. '*You* could have come to visit *us*, Mother. It is not so very far.'

'But your father, Flora.' She spoke in hushed tones. 'You know what he's like.'

'Maybe, Mother, he is the way he is because no one has ever stood up to him. Did you *ask* him if you could visit us?'

Lachlan hid his astonishment and his pride. Flora had said she no longer needed her family's forgiveness, but he hadn't realised she now had enough confidence to actually demand answers from her mother. Would her newfound bravado extend to challenging her father as well?

Lady Aberwyld flushed. 'I... No. I am sorry.' She

smiled tremulously at Lachlan. 'I am happy to see you, too, Mr McNeill. You both look well.'

Flora's expression softened, and she hugged her mother. 'Please call him Lachlan, Mother, and we are happy to see you, too.'

Lachlan greeted Flora's mother with a smile, content to remain in the background while Flora established her new relationship with her family, but he would stay vigilant until he saw what reception she received from her father.

'Where is everyone?'

'Your father is in bed. He's had a bit of a fever this past week, but he is recovering now.'

'And you didn't think to write and tell me, Mother? Did you not think I would care?'

Lady Aberwyld reddened. 'It was but a head cold that went to his lungs. It was not serious enough to worry you. I'll let Donald and the girls know you've come, but ye'd better see your father first. I'll go ahead and tell him you're here.'

Lord Aberwyld lay in his huge four-poster bed, propped up by pillows. He looked pale and drained, but he perked up when he saw Flora.

'Come over here, lassie, where I can see you.' His gaze flitted to Lachlan. 'How d'ye do, McNeill?'

Lachlan nodded, but stayed back, knowing Aberwyld was the sort of man who would converse with a husband about a wife even if the woman was there in front of him. Flora rounded the bed and sat on the chair while her mother stood at the foot of the bed. Lachlan remained by the door and watched closely for any hint of distress from his wife.

'Ye're a sight for sore eyes, lassie.' Aberwyld raised

his hand and Flora held it. 'I'm pleased ye've come to visit the auld place.'

'It is you I've come to see, Father. You and Mother and the rest of my family.'

'Ye always were a good daughter.'

Flora's lips curved into a wry smile as she met Lachlan's eyes. 'You have not always thought of me as such, Father.'

Aberwyld's eyes narrowed. 'That is in the past, now.'

Her chin lifted. Lachlan recognised the sign. His wife was not about to meekly accept her father's edict and Lachlan stepped forward, ready to intervene.

'Not for me, Father.'

'What d'ye mean?' A fearsome frown creased Aberwyld's forehead.

'I am speaking of the entire family's treatment of me after I refused Galkirk. And *that* was due to your edict that I must suffer for not blindly obeying you. You did not care that he tried to force himself on me. I lived a full year isolated and alone in the middle of my own family. Have you any idea how horrible that was for me? How insignificant and unloved I felt?'

Lady Aberwyld gasped, her hand to her mouth.

'We needed Galkirk's money. Have *you* any idea what a struggle it's been to try to keep the estates and this family going, and the tenants on their farms?'

'Perhaps,' Flora said, 'you might have told me of that struggle and allowed me to help. I had ideas, but you only ever listened to Donald, even though his ideas were often ludicrous. You never gave the slightest consideration to *any* of my suggestions. I always felt as though you never even heard me.'

'I am sorry that's how you felt, lass.' Aberwyld's voice was gruff and Lachlan could see what an effort it was for such a proud man to apologise to his daughter. 'But Donald will be clan leader—it's important he grows up strong and decisive. I don't regret raising him that way and he's come up with a winning scheme now—English tourists paying to sleep in the same bedchamber the Queen and Prince Albert slept in.'

Anger flashed across Flora's face and Lachlan recalled her telling him of that same idea—*her* idea—and one her father had rejected. But Lady Aberwyld had stiffened at her husband's words and now she spoke out before Flora could.

'That idea was Flora's, Malcolm.' She looked nervous but determined. 'She suggested it earlier this year.'

Aberwyld scowled. 'Well, I canna say I recall. But the *boat* was definitely Donald's idea.'

'Aye, it was.' Flora's brother had come unnoticed into the room. The young man had filled out a little since their wedding—or was it just that he held himself with more confidence? 'And Mother is right, Father. I did get the idea of the Queen's bedchamber from Flora.'

Flora came to greet her brother and Lachlan saw her surprise when Donald pulled her into a hug.

'It's good to see you, Sis.' His voice was gruff. 'I feared we wouldna see ye again after the way we treated you.'

'I've missed you all.' Flora's eyes were bright with unshed tears. 'And thank you for Bandit, Donald. Knowing you'd done that for me... It—it meant the world to me. Truly. It gave me hope we might one day be a family again. I hope this might be a new start and that you will all fully accept me and Lachlan from now on.'

Lady Aberwyld put her arm around Flora. 'We will, won't we, Malcolm? And Aileen and Mairi cannot wait to see you. I thought it would be too tiring for your father to have you all in here at once so I told them to wait.' She bent a stern look on Donald. 'Donald, however, saw fit to ignore that.'

'Sorry, Mother. But I was listening at the door and I heard Father talk about the new scheme and I didn't want Flora to think I was claiming her idea as my own. I apologise to you, too, Flora,' he added. 'I was always jealous of your quick wits and that's the truth. I felt I lagged two steps behind you when it came to thinking of new ideas and I'm sorry you didn't get the credit you should have done. It wasn't until you'd gone that I realised what you meant to me.'

Flora beamed at him. 'Thank you, Donald. You cannot know how much it means to me to hear you say that. Now, what is this talk of a boat?'

'The idea of taking in tourists came from you, Flora, but then I tried to think about what they would want to do while they were here. So I came up with the idea of buying a boat to take them up the coast and across to the islands. The English love all of that, so I understand. And it means they will stay here for more than just the one night if we put on some day excursions. We already have bookings for next year.'

'It's a grand idea, Donald,' said Lachlan. 'And—' he flashed a grin at Flora '—as Flora has told me your kinsman—Sandy, was it?—no longer supplies the castle with whisky, will you consider using our Carnmore Whisky for your guests? We have brought a couple of bottles with us, so you can try it before you commit.'

'It'll have to be good to compete with Sandy's brew,' Aberwyld growled, but he winked at Flora as he spoke and Lachlan's heart expanded as he saw her joy.

'We will give it a try.' Donald extended his hand to

Lachlan. 'It's good to see you again, McNeill. I hope you're treating my sister well?'

'You'd be better asking that question of Flora, Mc-Crieff. But I can confirm that the reverse is true and that your sister treats me very well indeed.'

'And likewise,' said Flora, with a smile. 'Now, Mother. Where are my sisters? I cannot wait to see them again.'

Watching Lachlan gradually unbend in the company of her family that evening made Flora even more determined to heal the rift between herself and Anna, for his sake. They would spend the next day at Castle McCrieff, but must return to Lochmore on Saturday to prepare for their trip to Glasgow on Monday. They were to stay with Tessa and William rather than at a hotel and Flora also planned to call upon Anna with a plan to involve her more closely in their lives. The success of their visit to Flora's family had given her another idea—one to convince Lachlan that he now truly belonged to a large and settled family.

After breakfast on the day they were due to travel home, she slipped away to her father's room where he was now strong enough to sit in his chair. She couldn't help but feel some of the old trepidation whenever she was with Father but she tried hard to conceal it and, to her surprise, he seemed to respect her for standing up to him.

'I have an invitation for you, Father. I should like you all to come to Lochmore for Hogmanay. It's a few weeks away yet and you should be strong enough to travel by then.'

'You want the McCrieff laird to see in the New Year on Lochmore land?'

'A McCrieff is mistress there now,' she reminded him.

He grunted, and scowled down at the bedcovers.

'Well? Will you come?'

'Aye.' He sighed, then brightened. 'Ye're right! It'll be a tonic to see a McCrieff as mistress.'

'Thank you. But please don't tell Lachlan. It is to be a surprise—I'm hoping his sister and nephew will agree to come.'

'Aye. We'll be there. I'll tell your mother.'

Flora kissed his whiskery cheek. 'Thank you. I'm happy we're all friends again.' Dare she push him one step further? 'It's important to heal family rifts, is it not? Which reminds me—I met Tessa several weeks ago. My Aunt Tessa.' Her pulse kicked as he glared at her, but she did not back down. 'She asked after you.'

She waited. After a few minutes' silence, her father growled, 'Is she well?'

'She is.'

'And William Anderson?'

So all these years he'd remembered the name of the man she married? Perhaps there was hope. 'Him, too.'

'Good.'

She wasn't quite brave enough to ask him about the skeleton in the tower. Not yet—it was more important to reconcile the living first. The dead could wait. But she *would* ask Father. One day. Because she still felt that urge to find out the truth.

'Goodbye, Father. And make sure you get well for Hogmanay. I'll see you then.'

She ran down the stairs to find Lachlan waiting in the hall, surrounded by yapping puppies.

'What's all this?'

'Sal's newest litter,' Donald said. Sal was Bandit's mother. 'D'ye fancy another terrier, Sis? Lachlan?'

'No,' they said in unison and laughed as their eyes met.

'One mischief-maker in our lives is more than enough, thank you,' said Lachlan. He took Flora's hand, his smile warm. 'Let's go home.'

Three days later, Glasgow

Flora called upon Anna in her new home while Lachlan attended a shareholders' meeting for the railway. Anna showed Flora the changes she had made—she now had three new lodgers—and, after peeping in on Davy, who was taking a nap, they settled in the sitting room.

'Lachy chose not to come with you?'

'Lachlan doesn't know I am here, Anna. I have a favour to ask but, first, I have a proposition for you.'

'Proposition?'

'Yes.' Flora was determined to make this work. 'Lachlan and I plan to set up a charity to help women who have fallen on hard times.'

She explained briefly her idea of setting up a clothing business and employing widowed or abandoned mothers as seamstresses, allowing them to work from home, giving them an income and allowing them to look after their children at the same time.

'We need someone in the city who understands their lives, someone we can trust to manage the charity and who won't cheat the women. I hoped you might take on the role.'

Anna frowned. 'Why me?'

'You have the experience of the pressures these women face—they will respect that and trust you. I can think of no better person to oversee this end of the charity.'

'And why have ye not told my brother of this proposition.'

'I want to surprise him. I know he'll be delighted if you agree to work with us.'

And she didn't want Lachlan to be hurt if Anna flatly refused to be involved. She had already sworn to pay back her brother every penny he'd spent on her behalf—even insisting on paying him rent for this house.

'You would be paid, of course,' said Flora, 'and Lachlan intends to buy or lease a house to offer a refuge to any woman who finds herself in difficulties, until she is earning enough to afford a roof over her head. If you will agree, he will look for a house near here, so it's easier for you to manage.'

She could see Anna's struggle in her eyes.

'It will take a while to set everything in place,' Flora continued. 'But I would be more confident if I knew I could rely on you.'

'Verra well. I'll do it.'

'Thank you!' Tension seeped from her shoulders and neck. Her plan was coming together. 'Lachlan will be thrilled. I must go. Do you think Davy is awake yet? I'd love to see him before I go.'

'I'll go and fetch him.'

Within minutes, Anna reappeared at the sitting room door carrying a tousled Davy, rubbing at his eyes. As soon as he saw Flora, however, he wriggled out of Anna's arms.

'Bandit? Where's Bandit?'

'He's at home, Davy,' said Flora. 'He wouldn't like the city. He's not used to it.'

The little boy pouted. 'Want Bandit.'

'He never stops pestering me for a dog,' said Anna.

Flora's thoughts flew to Sal and her litter. 'Would you allow him to have one?'

'Aye, I intend to get him one. Your Bandit did him more good to start him talking again than any of our efforts.'

'Well, in that case, why don't you bring him to the castle for Hogmanay to visit Bandit? That was the favour I meant to ask—it's important for families to be together to see in the New Year.' She would write to Donald and ask him to bring one of Sal's pups with him for Davy. 'My aunt and uncle, Tessa and William, are coming, plus my parents, brother and two sisters. Please say you'll come, Anna. It wouldn't be the same without you and Davy.' And she genuinely meant it. Their family would not be complete without Anna and Davy. 'But it is to be a surprise for Lachlan so don't say anything to him, will you?

'And my aunt, Tessa, said you could travel to Lochmore with them if you like. Although, I should warn you—my father hasn't spoken to his sister for years, so sparks might fly when he finds out she is there.'

'Ah, well now...' Anna grinned '...we're used to sparks flying between brother and sister, are we not, Flora?'

Chapter Twenty-Two

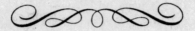

Noon, New Year's Eve

The message from Gregor couldn't have come at a worse time.

Since Anna and Davy had left Lochmore, Lachlan had worked hard to conceal his dejection from Flora. He knew, with his head, that he must look forward to the future. But his heart wasn't quite ready to let go of his dream of having his family around him.

He had promised Flora that they would spend this last day of the old year together and that business would not intrude, but they had no sooner returned from a bracing walk on the beach and settled by the fire than a messenger from the distillery rode up to the castle with a note to say Gregor needed Lachlan urgently.

Lachlan hesitated. He longed to reply to Gregor that he must deal with the problem himself. Flora came to him and put her hands in his.

'You must go.'

'But—'

'Go. You know you won't rest if you don't find out what is wrong. And I shall insist on your undivided attention later.'

She smiled a mischievous smile and tiptoed up to press soft lips to his cheek. His heart tumbled in his chest. He was so lucky—a beautiful wife, a lovely home, business going well. Anna had even agreed to help them manage their charity, meaning Lachlan got to see more of her. He still missed having her and Davy here, though, and seeing them every day. If only they had stayed, life would be perfect indeed.

He wrapped his arms around Flora's waist and kissed her lips. Thoroughly. Her scent calmed him and excited him at the same time and he again blessed his good fortune and yet…and yet…still there lingered that fear that it was all too good for him. That Flora would, one day, reject him and leave, just as Anna had.

His eyes roamed her beautiful face as she smiled up at him. She was kind and honest and fun…but did she love him? She had never said so and he longed to hear those words on her lips. Her gaze slipped sideways, then she jerked out of his embrace. His breath hitched in alarm.

'Oh, for goodness sake. *Get down*, Bandit!'

He followed the direction of Flora's exasperated stare, then burst out laughing when he saw the cause of her distraction. How stupid for panic to steal his breath, even for a split second.

Bandit was on his hind legs, nosing at the wrapped sweet treats that still hung suspended by colourful ribbons from the branches of their Christmas tree. Lachlan had never heard of such a thing as a Christmas tree before, but Flora had assured him it was a tradition that Prince Albert had brought to Britain from his homeland of Germany and that the practice was increasingly popular. They cut a young fir from the steep slope at the side of Loch Arris and decorated it together on Christmas Eve with ribbons, candles and those sweet treats, wrapped in silver and gold paper, and Flora had insisted all their decorations—including the swags of fir, dressed with berries, ribbons and candles, that adorned the downstairs rooms—should remain in place until Twelfth Night.

But Hogmanay was the main celebration in Scotland. A traditional Scottish feast of haggis, neeps and tatties was already being prepared and custom said that whatever you did at midnight as the New Year began, you would continue to do throughout the year. And Lachlan could think of nothing he would rather do than hold his wife in his arms and kiss her senseless.

'Go, my darling. That message sounded urgent.'

It was something and nothing, he thought as he rode home three hours later. Why Gregor couldn't have managed the repair himself he didn't know, but together they had fixed the valve and then Lachlan rode the eight miles home again. The first flakes of snow fluttered down when he was but a mile from the castle and he urged Copper, his chestnut gelding, into a trot. His mood lifted. This was his first New Year with Flora and, although it would be quiet, at least it would be better than last year when the celebration had passed Lachlan by without him even noticing.

He dismounted at the stable yard and handed Copper over to a groom before crossing the inner bailey to the castle. The front door opened and Drummond said, 'You're home just in time, sir.' He nodded skywards. 'It looks like it means business, no?'

'It does indeed.' Lachlan stripped off his greatcoat, hat and gloves and handed them to his butler. 'Where is Lady Flora?'

'In the drawing room, sir.'

He strode across the hall, pushed open the drawing room door, walked in and stopped dead.

'Uncle Lachy!' A small solid body cannoned into his knees and he instinctively scooped Davy into his arms.

Davy wriggled impatiently. 'Come see!'

Lachlan could barely believe his eyes. The drawing room was ablaze with light and colour and full, so it seemed, of people. His gaze sought Flora. She approached him slowly, her hands outstretched and with a loving smile.

'Our family have come to celebrate Hogmanay with us, Lachlan.'

He swept the room again, identifying the faces. Anna, of course, as Davy was here—a glass of wine in hand and looking more relaxed than he had seen her since their reunion—sitting with Flora's mother; Tessa and her brother, Lord Aberwyld, standing close together, his arm around her; William, standing slightly apart from the rest as he watched Tessa and her brother; Donald, Aileen and Mairi, sitting in a circle on the floor over by the window with Bandit and—

'Come *see*!'

He winced at that shout, so close to his ear. With an extra-determined wiggle, Davy squirmed free of Lachlan, grabbed his hand and tugged him towards the brown and white puppy that was the centre of attention.

'Patch! He's mine!' Davy stooped to grab the puppy, but Donald stopped him.

'Gentle now, laddie. He's much smaller than you. You'll hurt him. Here, hold him like this.'

Lachlan, still speechless, looked at Flora.

'I hope you approve, my darling. We are having a proper family celebration for Hogmanay…the first of many, I hope.'

Her face glowed with joy and that made him happy. All he wanted, he realised, was for her to be happy. All the time. It had crept up on him almost without him noticing— her happiness was more important to him than anything. *Anything.*

The unfamiliar sensation started way down inside, in his stomach. Swirling, tightening, swelling, as though something was trying to battle its way up and out through his strangely painful throat. His vision wavered—Flora's dear face blurred and his eyes and nose stung and burned. His chest heaved and he only just managed to stop the sob from erupting. To hide his reaction—his emotion— he grabbed Flora and hugged her to him, bending his neck to nuzzle her hair that smelled of orange blossom.

'Thank you.' He put his lips to her ear. These words were for her alone. 'I love you, my sweet, darling wife.' His voice cracked, but he felt a sense of peace he had finally spoken his true feelings aloud.

Flora wrapped her arms around his waist and hugged him hard before leaning back and lifting his chin with her fingers.

'Lachlan? Are you...?'

He put his mouth to her ear again. 'Happy tears.' He finally understood. 'They are happy tears.'

After all the frantic preparations for so many visitors— and the need to keep it all secret from Lachlan—Flora felt she could finally breathe easily as she climbed the stairs to rest a short while before dressing for dinner. Their family was all here and, amazingly enough, in harmony. After Muriel helped her disrobe she stripped off her chemise and donned her cream-silk dressing robe before going to Lachlan's bedchamber, where he was in his shirt sleeves. When he saw her, he dismissed Murray.

'Why are you not resting, sweetheart? Are you not tired?'

She went to him and folded herself against his warm body.

'Did you like your surprise, Lachlan?'

He smiled as he loosened the belt of her robe and slid his hands inside. Shivers erupted in the wake of his touch. As he pulled her closer she could feel his desire for her as his erection pressed against the soft roundness of her belly.

'I did.' He nuzzled her hair. 'It was a lovely gift to make this celebration very special. It is a long time since I felt part of a large family and I like that feeling.'

He lowered his head, but she raised her hands higher, framing his face, stopping him from kissing her. He gave a puzzled smile.

'I have another gift for you.'

He grinned wolfishly and flexed his hips. 'I know.'

She held him in place, resisting that near-overwhelming urge to feel him inside her. Their gazes fused, heat swirling in the dark depths of his. She would never grow tired of his lovemaking and the pleasure he brought her.

'Not that. This. I love you, Lachlan, my husband. I love you with all of my heart and soul.'

His eyes sheened. He sighed, smiled and then he seized her lips. They saw out the old year and she knew that, after midnight, they would see in the new.

Epilogue

Midsummer's Day, 1849— Lochmore Castle

Flora watched with pride as crowds flocked along the path to the clifftop meadow for the Carnmore Games— the first of a long tradition, she and Lachlan hoped. They had wanted to establish an annual event at Lochmore and Joane and Benneit—who had returned from his travels in January as planned—had told them of the Solstice Ball his father had thrown at Lochmore Castle every year. Lachlan and Flora, however, thought a ball was too exclusive. They wanted a gathering where everyone, whatever their class, could come to Lochmore and have a day of fun.

Flora had suggested a gathering for the local area and for all the people who worked for them. There would be food and drink, music and dancing, plus competitions based on the old clan games held in the past to pick the strongest and fastest clan members to act as bodyguards and couriers for the chieftains. The contests would include running races and tug o' war plus some of the traditional heavy events: the caber toss, using the trunk of a straight pine tree; the stone put, throwing smooth round stones, sourced from a river bed; and the weight throw, using a lead weight with a handle attached by a short chain. As the bagpipes wailed—stirring her blood as they always did—and she saw the happy crowds, many of the men in traditional Highland dress, their women with plaid shawls or dresses, a huge bubble of contentment swelled inside her and her eyes teared up.

She dashed the moisture away with an embarrassed smile—she was strangely tearful lately.

Happy tears.

This year had been the happiest of her life so far and there was greater joy to come.

The past week had been hectic with all the preparations, but it had been worth it. Tents and stalls selling all manner of refreshments, treats and trinkets ringed the meadow and in the centre was a space where the competitions would take place. Lachlan had arranged transport for his distillery workers to attend and had also chartered a steamer to bring friends and family, together with the women who were already benefitting from the McNeill Foundation and working as seamstresses to support themselves and their children. Flora and Anna had worked hard to set everything in place for the Foundation, including a warehouse where shoppers could purchase their clothing, and they were confident the business would eventually be self-funding.

Benneit, in his capacity as Duke of Lochmore, was to officially declare the Games open and award the prizes, and he and Joane and their entire family were present, down to little Louisa. And all of Flora's family, including Tessa and William, had also come to join in the fun. She had watched with trepidation as Father had gone straight over to Benneit as soon as he arrived, but then she had breathed a sigh of relief as the two men shook hands and shared a wee dram of Carnmore Whisky. In no time at all they were on the best of terms, agreeing that clan feuds were best left in the past where they belonged and Flora dared to hope that, very soon, she would finally brave her father's wrath and ask him for the truth about the lonely skeleton in the Great Tower at Castle McCrieff.

Two arms encircled her from behind and she leaned back into Lachlan's solid strength, breathing in his familiar musky male scent.

'You should be sitting down,' he grumbled into her ear. 'You work too hard.'

'I will shortly.' She turned to face him. 'We've been blessed with the weather, have we not? Apart from these dratted midges.'

She waved her hand in front of her face to disperse the cloud of biting insects that clustered around them.

'At least it's fresher here on the clifftop than down in the glens or around the marshes by the Canal. They'll be nigh-on intolerable down there.' He touched her cheek, his dark eyes warm. 'But not even midges will be allowed to spoil my day.' He inhaled, his chest expanding as he gazed around the meadow and then up to the sky before returning his gaze to Flora. 'I am a very happy man. Happy and proud.'

She smiled up at him. 'I am glad to hear that, for so am I. It is not only the weather we are blessed with, is it, my love?'

'No, indeed.' He pressed his warm lips to hers and she jerked away in surprise.

'Lachlan! We are in public!'

'I could not care less.' He cradled her face and kissed her again.

Neither could I.

She returned his kiss, her tongue sliding against his, relishing the familiar tug at her core as her body prepared for his. Her desire for her gorgeous husband—no longer a stern, unfathomable stranger, but familiar and loving and kind and generous—grew stronger with every passing day.

He released her mouth and smiled down at her. 'I could not care less,' he repeated, 'because I want the whole world to know that I am in love with my wife.' His eyes turned serious. 'I thought I only needed a wife for my business and I could not see how alone I was. I was blessed when I married you, Flora McNeill—you healed both of our families to become one but, more importantly, you healed my heart and you healed my soul. I never imagined I could be so happy—I adore our family, but I need only you. You are my world...*you* are my family.'

Flora smiled and placed his hand on her belly.

'*We* are your family, Lachlan.'

She waited, watching until she saw the understanding grow in his dark eyes.

'Always. You will never be alone again.'

* * * * *

*If you enjoyed this story be sure to check out
the next books in The Lochmore Legacy miniseries*

Unlaced by the Highland Duke
by Lara Temple
A Runaway Bride for the Highlander
by Elisabeth Hobbes
Secrets of a Highland Warrior
by Nicole Locke

*And also be sure to check out
The Beauchamp Betrothals miniseries
by Janice Preston, starting with*

Cinderella and the Duke